London Hospital Midwives

Delivering miracles and meeting their match!

In Queen Victoria Hospital's maternity wing, midwives and friends Esther, Carly, Chloe and Izzy deliver miracles every day—but haven't found their own happily-ever-afters!

All that's about to change when some unexpected arrivals of the tall, dedicated and handsome kind shake up the maternity ward and the lives—and hearts—of these amazing midwives!

Cinderella and the Surgeon by Scarlet Wilson
Miracle Baby for the Midwife by Tina Beckett
Reunited by Their Secret Daughter by Emily Forbes
A Fling to Steal Her Heart by Sue MacKay

All available now!

Dear Reader,

Writing is often a fairly solitary pursuit. While I have fabulous editorial support, the editors are in another hemisphere, and it's not possible to chat about my books face-to-face. So I really embrace the chance to write as part of a team on occasion.

This book is one of four in the London Hospital Midwives quartet. I did enjoy the process even if we still weren't able to get together as we are scattered around the globe—Scotland, the USA, Australia and New Zealand! You might see a bit of that international flavor reflected in our stories.

If you haven't read all four books, look out for them:

Book 1 *Cinderella and the Surgeon* by Scarlet Wilson
Book 2 *Miracle Baby for the Midwife* by Tina Beckett
Book 4 *A Fling to Steal Her Heart* by Sue MacKay

I'd love to hear from you if you've enjoyed this story or any of my others. You can visit my website, emily-forbesauthor.com, or drop me a line at emilyforbes@internode.on.net.

Emily

REUNITED BY THEIR
SECRET DAUGHTER

———

EMILY FORBES

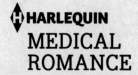

HARLEQUIN

MEDICAL
ROMANCE

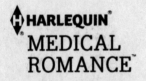

HARLEQUIN®
MEDICAL
ROMANCE™

Recycling programs
for this product may
not exist in your area.

ISBN-13: 978-1-335-14925-1

Reunited by Their Secret Daughter

Harlequin Enterprises ULC
22 Adelaide St. West, 40th Floor
Toronto, Ontario M5H 4E3, Canada
www.Harlequin.com

Printed in U.S.A.

Emily Forbes is an award-winning author of Harlequin Medical Romance novels. She has written over twenty-five books and has twice been a finalist in the Australian Romantic Book of the Year Award, which she won in 2013 for her novel *Sydney Harbor Hospital: Bella's Wishlist*. You can get in touch with Emily at emilyforbes@internode.on.net, or visit her website at emily-forbesauthor.com.

For Scarlet, Tina and Sue,
my fellow London Hospital Midwives authors.
What a team. We did it!

Love,
Emily

Praise for
Emily Forbes

"Ms. Forbes has delivered a delightful read in
this book where emotions run high because of
everything this couple go through on their journey
to happy ever after...and where the chemistry
between this couple was strong; the romance was
delightful and had me loving these two together."
—*Harlequin Junkie* on *Rescued by the Single Dad*

CHAPTER ONE

'*HAPPY BIRTHDAY, DEAR LILY! Happy Birthday to you!*'

Chloe Larson blinked back tears as Lily blew out the candles on her birthday cake. She couldn't believe she had a three-year-old daughter.

She pulled the candles from the cake and picked up the knife. 'Shall I help you cut it up?' she asked.

'I want Granny to help me,' Lily said.

Chloe tried not to be hurt. Ever since Chloe had found out she was pregnant at the age of twenty-four and had chosen to be a single mother, her own mother had been supportive. Chloe knew she couldn't have raised Lily without her help, and she tried not to mind when Lily turned to Susan as easily as she turned to Chloe, but sometimes she wished that life had been different.

She held back a sigh as she passed the knife

to her mum. There was no point in wishing for something that wasn't to be.

'Make a wish, Lily,' Susan said as she guided her granddaughter's hand to slice through the rainbow cake.

'Don't touch the bottom, Lil,' Chloe's brother Tom prompted.

Lily carefully lifted pieces of cake onto pink paper plates. 'Uncle Tom gets one first,' she said as she handed cake to her guests. 'When will Uncle Guy get here?'

'You saw him this morning, Lil. He's working tonight. We'll have to save him a piece.'

'Can you take me for another ride now, Uncle Tom?' Lily asked as she put a final piece of cake aside for Guy.

Chloe's brothers had given Lily a pink bike, with streamers dangling from the handles and a set of stabilisers on the back, for her birthday and Lily had spent most of the day riding up and down the driveway with Tom close behind.

'Sure.'

At twenty-one, Tom had plenty of energy, despite his job as a paramedic, and he doted on Lily as all Chloe's family did. Chloe knew how lucky she was. People said it took a village to raise a child, and Chloe was grateful to her mother and brothers for their support.

And to her girlfriends. She had a lot to be thankful for.

'Come and watch me, Granny.'

Lily skipped outside followed by Tom and Susan, leaving Chloe inside with two of her best friends.

'Okay, who will join me in a glass of wine or a G&T? Esther?'

'Wine, please,' Esther replied as Carly, who was in the early stages of pregnancy, said, 'No wine for me, but I wouldn't say no to another piece of cake.'

'What would you wish for, Chloe, if it was your birthday?' Esther asked her when she returned with the wine and Carly cut more cake. 'How about your own happily ever after?'

Chloe looked sideways at Esther. The three women had been friends since they'd undertaken their midwifery training at the Queen Victoria together, and along with Isabella, who was currently overseas, the four of them had formed a tight-knit unit and sometimes Chloe was sure they could read each other's minds. But surely Esther wouldn't have guessed that Chloe was wishing for a different life?

'I'm already happy,' Chloe replied. She always insisted that she was happy with her life. She'd made a choice and she didn't regret it, even if it hadn't always been easy.

'How about satisfied, then? Couldn't you do with a white knight to come riding into your world?'

That was the trouble now that Carly and Esther had each found their perfect match and were deeply in love—they were both soon to be married and wanted everyone else to have their own happily ever after. But serious relationships were not for her; in her experience they only led to heartache. She'd be happy for Esther and Carly—she *was* happy for them—and she'd be a supportive friend, but she wouldn't make the mistake of believing she could have her own happily ever after again. She'd been in love once before and it hadn't ended the way she'd hoped.

'I'm fine,' she insisted.

Her life was busy and she was rarely alone even if she was sometimes lonely. Her days were spent either at work in Accident and Emergency at the Queen Victoria Hospital where she was surrounded by patients and colleagues or at home with her daughter. Home was her childhood house where Chloe's youngest brother, Tom, and her mother also lived. Chloe had never moved out, although that had been her intention. She'd finished school and stayed home while she completed her nursing and then midwifery training but her unexpected pregnancy had derailed her plans and here she was, three years later, still living in her mother's house.

It sounded depressing, it sounded as if she hadn't achieved a great deal, but she paid rent and her share of the bills. She was a flat-mate in a sense, not a free boarder. Plus she had a good relationship with her mother and Lily benefited from having family around— she loved her granny and her uncles. The arrangement suited everyone and Chloe was happy enough. She couldn't deny that sometimes she wished for companionship, and yes, sometimes she wished for more sex too, but she didn't believe in one-night stands and she didn't believe in people's ability to maintain long-term monogamous relationships so she was caught between a rock and a hard place. It would take someone pretty special to make her believe in happily ever after again. She thought she might have missed her chance at finding her 'one.'

'How long since you've been on a date?' Esther asked.

'It's been a while,' she admitted.

'Can you be more specific?' Carly asked with a smile.

'November.'

'*November!* It's already March!'

'I know. But everyone is busy over Christmas and then, in the middle of winter, I can't be bothered going out.'

'Maybe you should try online dating,' Carly suggested. 'At least that way you can start the process from home. You can peruse the menu in your pyjamas, so to speak.'

But Chloe had heard too many bad stories about online dating. She wanted to feel that spark of attraction from seeing someone in the flesh. She knew that existed. It had happened to her before. She didn't want to flick through online sites judging people on their photoshopped looks or their fabricated profiles and she certainly didn't want people judging *her* anonymously. She shook her head.

'You should think about it, Chlo,' Esther said. 'I'd love you to bring a date to my wedding.'

Esther had told her on numerous occasions she was welcome to bring a guest but Chloe couldn't imagine where she'd find someone she wanted to be her 'plus one.'

'I could ask Harry if he knows anyone or maybe you'll meet someone at the wedding,' Esther said before turning to Carly. 'Or maybe Adem has some nice single friends?'

Chloe's blood ran cold at the idea of being paraded around to all the single men. 'I know you mean well, but I'm okay on my own. Really.'

Esther and Carly both looked a little sheepish. 'Sorry. You know we love you and we just want you to be happy.'

'I am,' she insisted again. 'Don't say anything to Harry or Adem on my behalf but I'll let you know if I change my mind about a date. Okay?'

Maybe she should take a date with her, even if it was just someone to provide a shield, some protection, if necessary. But she had no idea where she would find such a person.

Chloe put Lily's favourite bedtime story book down and wriggled carefully out of her daughter's bed, trying not to disturb her. She pulled the covers up and took a moment to watch her sleeping.

Lily was the spitting image of her at the same age. Her riot of strawberry blond curls fanned across the pillow framing her round face. A scattering of freckles ran over her nose, little dark spots on her pale skin. She had one arm thrown up beside her head and Chloe knew there was a graze on her bony elbow and another one on her knee. She reached out and touched one of Lily's curls. Chloe had always hated her own hair, especially as a teenager, and the minute she could afford to she had bought a straightening iron and had dyed her hair blond, but now she loved her daughter's strawberry curls. Chloe still dyed her hair, although she had given up straightening it except on occasion. Straightening her hair took time and that was a luxury she didn't have much of any more.

The only differing feature between her and her daughter at the age of three was the colour of their eyes. Chloe's were dark brown, Lily's were grey, and in Chloe's opinion Lily's were far more striking especially in contrast to her pale auburn curls.

She searched her daughter's face looking for any resemblance to the man who had fathered her. She liked to think there was something of him in Lily but as more time passed it was becoming harder to remember all the little details. Lily definitely had her father's grey eyes but she couldn't see those while Lily slept. She wondered if Lily ever wished that her father was around. Was something missing in her life? She seemed happy enough and she had good male role models but was that the same thing?

Chloe knew it wasn't. Chloe and her younger brothers had been raised by their mother after their father had died when Chloe was seven. Chloe loved her mum and she knew she'd done a brilliant job raising three kids on her own but that had never stopped Chloe from missing her father. Lily had never met her father; maybe that would be enough to stem those feelings of loss, but Chloe doubted it. It might not matter to Lily now but what about when she got older?

She wondered for the thousandth time what had happened to Lily's father. To Xander.

To the man who had captured her heart in the Australian outback four years ago.

He had looked like a blond Nordic god and she'd known from the moment she'd met him that he was damaged, wounded, but he was gorgeous, irresistible, and she'd been certain she could handle him. She'd been on a study exchange with the Australian flying doctor service and hadn't been looking for anything more than a holiday romance.

Initially everything had been fine. Manageable. On paper, their affair looked perfect. She was young and footloose and Xander had just been through an acrimonious divorce. Neither of them had been looking for anything serious and they'd both been happy to have a light-hearted liaison, something to satisfy their mutual physical attraction and desires. Their time together had lasted less than four weeks. That was all the time she had left in Australia. It was enough time to have some fun but not long enough for heartache.

At the end of the month she hadn't been ready to leave but she figured she'd forget about him in time. A holiday romance wasn't meant to be for ever. She missed him but she figured she'd get over it.

She would focus on her career, on getting a contract with the Air Ambulance Service, and Xander Jameson would become part of her past. A memory to take out and relive from time to time.

But she hadn't expected the emptiness that gnawed away at her. The ache that felt like a lump of lead in her chest. She'd never fully given her heart to anyone—in her experience men had a wandering eye and had trouble staying faithful, and she protected her heart zealously, careful not to give it away—but Xander had caught her by surprise.

She certainly hadn't planned to fall in love. In her experience love didn't last. Her parents' marriage had crumbled under the weight of her father's infidelity and Chloe's one semi-serious relationship at the age of twenty-one had suffered the same fate. In her experience falling in love only led to heartache. But that didn't stop it from happening to her.

She hadn't counted on meeting Xander.

And she hadn't counted on falling pregnant.

She had been back in London for a month before she realised. At least that situation explained her unexpected feelings. She wasn't in love, she told herself, just overwhelmed by a flood of hormones.

She tried to contact Xander—she knew it was the right thing to do—but he'd disappeared.

She'd wanted to find him; despite her strong views on serious relationships and their longevity she let herself get carried away with a fantasy, creating all sorts of happily ever afters in her mind, and part of her hoped for a miraculous happy ending even though she knew there were no such guarantees.

She only realised when she was trying unsuccessfully to find him how little she really knew about him. They hadn't spent much time talking about anything important. She knew he'd grown up in Adelaide in South Australia but he had no social media identity and his work colleagues had either been unable or unwilling to give her any useful information. Her letters had been returned to sender, unopened. He seemed to have disappeared off the face of the earth.

But she had never stopped wondering if

her life would have been different if she'd found him.

Would he have wanted to make them a family?

He had told her his marriage had ended because his wife had wanted children and, although he'd never voiced the words, Chloe took that to mean that he didn't.

She'd been relieved in a way not to find him. What would he think of Lily? She was glad she hadn't had to find out. The decisions about her pregnancy were hers alone to make and her dreams of a happily ever after remained just dreams.

Once Lily was born she'd had no time to continue her search and she'd doused the flames of her dreams and focused on the job of raising her daughter. But she'd never forgotten him.

She sighed.

How could she forget him when she was reminded of him every day? Every time she looked into her daughter's eyes.

She'd tried to forget and she'd tried to convince herself she hadn't been in love with him. If anything, her experience with Xander was just more proof that everlasting love was not meant for her.

She had her daughter, her miracle, her precious Lily. That would have to be enough.

She left Lily's night light on and the door ajar as she slipped out of the room while her mind continued to wander. If she'd realised the consequences of their affair would she have been more cautious?

She loved her daughter and she had absolutely no regrets about having her. She was always going to keep the baby—her mum had raised three kids with minimal help and Chloe knew she could raise one. She had never considered giving Lily up. She had no regrets about the choices she had made but she did sometimes wonder about a different future.

Maybe the fact that Esther and Carly were both about to settle down and join the ranks of the happily married was making her reassess her own life. Maybe she did need to get out on the dating scene. Maybe she would like some company. Now that Lily was three maybe Chloe's life would calm down, perhaps she would get some time to herself, a day that wasn't all consumed by motherhood and her career. Perhaps there would be some time for her to have a social life beyond an occasional drink or dinner with Carly and Esther. Nothing serious—casual dating would be fine. She wasn't going to dream of anything more than that. She and Lily were fine on their own and she wasn't prepared to settle for anyone ordinary. It was better to be single than to be with someone who wasn't perfect for her. And for Lily.

Still she wondered if Xander could have been that person.

She had been on a few dates since Lily had been born but no one had lived up to her memory of Xander. She was sensible enough to realise that her memory may have altered over the years. She was remembering all the good things, looking at him through rose-tinted glasses, but he couldn't be perfect. Four weeks just hadn't been long enough for her to get annoyed by his flaws.

But what if she had found him?

Where would they be now?

She shook her head. She couldn't survive on 'what ifs.' Even if she'd found him, he might not have been the person she wanted him to be. They'd had amazing chemistry but who knew if that would have been enough to sustain a happy, long-term relationship. She was certainly none the wiser.

She was sure there was a simple explanation to Xander's apparent disappearance but, whatever it was, she'd never been able to find him and now, here she was, almost four years later, still single, and Lily was still without a father.

Should she let her girlfriends set her up? Chloe wondered as she hurried through A&E to fetch another bag of saline. Was that the answer?

The idea of going on a date wasn't completely unappealing but the logistics of it wasn't as simple. Most days after a long shift at work and then coming home to a toddler, she barely had the energy for housework. She couldn't imagine having the energy to get ready and dressed up for a date.

She returned to the treatment cubicle and her patient, pushing all thoughts of dating aside.

'All right, Penny, this should help you feel better,' she said as she connected the bag of saline to the drip.

'Can you tell me again what the doctor said is wrong with me?' Penny asked.

'You have a condition called hyperemesis gravidarium,' Chloe told her as she updated Penny's chart. 'It's a medical term for severe morning sickness that unfortunately doesn't just hit you in the morning. I know you feel awful and while it can be serious it's not life-threatening and it will pass.'

'When?'

'It's usually much better by about halfway through your pregnancy.'

'That's another three months away,' Penny groaned, and reached for the bowl and proceeded to vomit again. She'd presented to A&E in the late afternoon, badly dehydrated, having vomited all day.

Chloe held Penny's hair back from her face and took the bowl from her when she finished, swapping it with a cool, damp flannel.

'Is there anything I can do to make it stop?' Penny asked.

'Some expectant mums find that drinking your food instead of eating it can help,' said Chloe. 'Making shakes and smoothies for example and a diet high in protein and carbohydrates is better than a fatty diet. Ginger and vitamin B6 can also help.'

Scans had shown that Penny was pregnant with only one baby and blood tests hadn't detected a virus or anything else untoward. She had low blood pressure and a rapid pulse but the nausea and dehydration were the main concern.

'Does the vomiting harm the baby?'

'Vomiting itself isn't harmful but it is important not to ignore the symptoms. If you're unable to keep food down, then you're not getting the nutrition you need and neither is the baby and sometimes this can cause a low birthweight. You do need to take care of yourself.' Chloe didn't want to frighten Penny unnecessarily but it was important to stress that she needed to monitor her condition. 'A lot of pregnant women with this condition find they need regular fluid top-ups to combat the dehydration. Anti-nausea medication as well and, very occasionally, hospital admission. I'm going to give you the details for the Early Pregnancy Unit here at the hospital. It's open every day during office hours. That's the place to go if you're feeling unwell. You'll get seen faster than here in A&E and you're less likely to pick up any bugs. I think you should pop in there for a check-up in the next day or two as they will be able to suggest some strategies to help you through this.'

Chloe pulled a notebook from the pocket of her scrubs and wrote down the phone number and details for the EPU as well as the scientific term for Penny's diagnosis. As she tucked it into Penny's bag the A&E manager stuck her head into the cubicle.

'Chloe? The air ambulance has called for a midwife. Can you go with them?' Shirley asked. 'I'll reassign your patient.'

Chloe nodded. 'Penny's notes are up to date. She's all set for the moment.'

Chloe was one of three midwives who worked with the Air Ambulance Service on an as-needed basis. The service had their base on the top floor of the Queen Victoria Hospital with a rooftop helipad, and Chloe had applied for a position at the hospital specifically to work with the service. She loved the work and wished she could do it full time but that would mean doing general nursing and not midwifery. She didn't want to give that up so this was the compromise; she felt it gave her the best of both worlds.

She threw her gloves into the bin and hurried to the lift, not wanting to waste time. Protocol dictated that the crew would aim to take off within four minutes of receiving a call.

She got out one flight before the roof and stepped into the pair of orange overalls that were handed to her. She zipped them up over her scrubs and ran up the stairs and out onto the roof. She jogged across to where the helicopter sat on the helipad, its rotors turning. She ducked her head instinctively even though she wasn't tall enough for the blades to hit her and climbed into the chopper and took her seat. Neil, one of the two fire officers on deck, slid the door closed behind her.

She reached up and unhooked a helmet that was hanging above her head. She tugged the elastic band that tied her unruly curls into a ponytail lower down on her neck so she could pull the helmet on. Sitting opposite her was Rick, one of the service's paramedics.

She hadn't been called for a job in over a month and she felt the familiar thrill of nervousness and anticipation as she fastened her helmet strap and reached for her harness. She worked quickly, not taking the time to glance at the other seat where one of the doctors would be sitting, as she knew the pilot was waiting to lift off.

'Chloe, this is Dr Alexander Jameson.' She slid one arm into her harness as she heard Rick introduce her to a new doctor. 'He's covering for Eloise while she's off after her knee surgery.'

Chloe felt a shiver down her spine and her heart rate increased even as she told herself she'd misheard. She *must* have misheard. She'd been thinking about Xander and must have imagined Rick had said his name because why would he be *here*? She kept her head down, taking longer than usual to click her harness together.

'He's just come down from Wales.'

Chloe breathed out. He was Welsh. Not Australian. It wasn't him.

But when she lifted her head she was looking directly into a pair of familiar grey eyes.

It *was* him.

Xander.

Her vision blurred as everything around her shifted. She squeezed her eyes shut, trying to clear her vision, but when she opened them she found Xander still looking straight back at her.

His eyes ensnared hers and held her motionless and she felt the air rush from her lungs as if she'd been punched in the stomach.

She stared at him. At the helmet that covered his head but not his perfect oval face with its angular, high cheekbones. At his full lips that were outlined by designer stubble and at his forehead that was slightly creased. She remembered that expression; so often serious, he usually looked either like he carried the weight of the world on his shoulders or was deep in thought.

She wanted to reach over and smooth the crease from his brow.

His grey eyes, which still held a trace of sadness, were wide, framed by thick, dark blond lashes, and they stared straight into her soul.

How could she have forgotten how gorgeous he was?

She was immediately transported back to a hot Australian day, to the first time she saw him. He had the same effect on her today as he'd had then. She couldn't breathe. She couldn't think. She couldn't stop staring at him. From the moment she'd first laid eyes on him almost four years ago she'd fallen hard and she could feel herself tumbling again.

How could she have forgotten the intensity of her feelings?

She felt light-headed, dizzy, and was grateful that she was already sitting down.

She had spent months trying to find him. Months thinking of all the terrible things that could have happened to him and here he was, apparently fit and well, sitting in her chopper.

CHAPTER TWO

'XANDER, CHLOE IS one of our on-call midwives.' Rick was still introducing them as if they didn't already know each other. As if Chloe's world hadn't just tipped on its axis.

Her heart was racing and her hands were shaking. She tucked them into her lap, hoping Rick and Xander didn't notice her reaction.

'Chloe.' He nodded. Once. Briefly.

He didn't deny that he knew her and he didn't pretend that he was meeting her for the first time but he certainly didn't appear too thrilled. He gave her nothing. She consoled herself with the fact that it wasn't the time or place for a personal conversation.

Would he be expecting one?

He probably hadn't thought about her once in four years. He would have no idea that she thought of him daily. He would have no idea of the impact he had made on her life.

She studied him fleetingly, trying not to

stare again. The orange jumpsuit that was the uniform for air ambulance medical staff was not the most flattering shade but Xander wore it well. His face was slightly tanned, making her wonder where else he'd been. Surely he hadn't got a tan in Wales? His shoulders were still broad, his legs long and lean. He looked thinner than she recalled and she wondered if his hair, beneath the helmet, was as thick and blond as she remembered. Four years ago he had worn it swept to one side, always looking as if he'd just finished running his fingers through it.

When she had left him behind, they'd had no plans for anything to go beyond a brief holiday fling. He had no idea that she'd spent months trying to find him.

She pushed the memories of their time together aside, before they could come flooding back. She couldn't afford to be swamped by the past. She had a job to do.

She could be professional. She *was* professional.

She'd waited years to speak to Xander. She'd given up on ever finding him. She could wait a few more hours to catch up.

She turned to Rick, hoping he was the one with all the information about the job and focused on the task at hand.

'Where are we headed?' she asked.

'Stabbing. Domestic dispute. Thirty-year-old woman, fourth pregnancy, thirty-eight weeks. Paramedics are on site. The woman and her partner are both being treated for injuries. The woman is in labour.'

Chloe digested the scant information. Details about the job were relayed to them by the co-pilot, Jeff, and were usually minimal. She knew the job was likely to be complicated but that was normally the case. The air ambulance wasn't called for simple incidents. But they wouldn't be the first pre-hospital team at the scene and she knew more information would be forthcoming once they arrived. The team had plenty of emergency medicine experience between them and were used to gathering information as they went.

Out of habit she checked the supplies stashed in the seat pockets beside her while her mind wandered.

She could feel Xander's eyes on her but she didn't dare meet his gaze. She needed to collect her thoughts before she connected with him and checking the supplies gave her something to occupy her throughout the short flight.

She needed to control her nerves. She concentrated on counting supplies, willing her hands to stop shaking. She was equal parts excited, nervous and worried.

She needed to focus but she was dying to know what he was thinking. What had he been doing? How was he? Did he ever think of her? And what did his arrival mean for her? For them? For Lily?

It was only a few minutes before she felt the helicopter begin the left-hand bank turn and knew they had reached their destination. The pilot, Simon, would be giving Jeff a chance to identify a safe landing site.

The house was easy to find; from her seat Chloe could see an ambulance, a police car and a police van parked out the front.

The chopper landed on a vacant block that looked as if it may have once been a tennis court. A few kids scattered to the footpath as it descended but then hung around, mouths open and eyes wide, to watch the scene unfold.

Rick slid the door open as the chopper touched down. Chloe reached for one of the kit bags only to find Xander had reached for the same one. Their hands touched and as Xander's came to rest on top of hers she jerked hers away as if she'd been scalded. Her skin was on fire, her breathing rapid. She kept her gaze averted and picked up a second bag as she tried to get her nerves under control.

She strode off, carrying the bag, quickly putting some distance between them. She needed to keep him out of her line of sight while she pulled herself together.

Two policemen emerged as they approached the house and between them Chloe could see a man in handcuffs. The husband? The police officers pushed on his head, forcing him into the back of their van before slamming the door. She gave him a cursory glance as she walked past before following Rick into the property.

The house was identical in appearance to several others in the street. A small front garden in need of some attention separated the house from the street. A short flight of steps led to the front door set in a narrow two-storey building. Chloe knew the floor plan—she'd been to many houses just like this one—and there was nothing to indicate from the outside what went on behind closed doors. Houses where domestic violence occurred could look like any other from the outside.

The front door opened into a tight hallway. There was a staircase on their right, an empty lounge on the left. Looking past Rick's shoulder Chloe could see a kitchen at the end of the hall. The air ambulance crew crowded into the small room.

A woman lay on the floor. Her shirt was ripped and bloodied and blood pooled on the linoleum. Her skin was pale and her breathing laboured. Two paramedics knelt on either side of her and one looked up as the team entered the room.

'This is Shania. Stab wound to the right chest.'

The paramedics had cut through the woman's top and the one who spoke was just finishing applying a dressing to the lateral side of the woman's chest.

'We've only just been able to get to her,' the paramedic continued. 'We had to wait for the police to subdue her partner.'

'She is complaining of difficulty breathing. She's hypoxic, absent air sounds,' the other paramedic said as he lifted the stethoscope that he'd been holding against the woman's chest. 'Rapid heart rate and sharp stabbing chest pain. I think she may have a tension pneumothorax.'

The air ambulance team all had their job roles emblazoned on the front left of their overalls. The paramedic holding the dressing reached into the kit that was beside her with her free hand and passed gloves to everyone before handing a stethoscope to Xander.

'She's thirty-eight weeks pregnant. Fourth pregnancy.' The paramedic repeated the information that the air ambulance team had already been given. 'She's in labour but we haven't had time to assess that.'

Xander knelt beside the woman. He placed the stethoscope against her chest and listened. Chloe was happy to defer to him. She knew there was no point asking the woman any questions about her labour until her chest pain was sorted. If she was having trouble breathing, she wouldn't want to talk. The woman's labour wasn't the priority. A tension pneumothorax was life-threatening.

Xander lifted his head. 'I need a large-bore needle, fourteen-gauge,' he said.

The paramedic handed him an angiocath along with an alcohol wipe. Xander swept the wipe across the woman's ribs and Chloe watched as he palpated for the intercostal space in the mid-clavicular line with slender fingers. His blond head was bent over the woman, the smooth skin on the back of his neck exposed as he leant over his patient.

He was talking to the woman, explaining what he was about to do.

He was calm and methodical. He worked

quickly but smoothly. There was no panic, no hurried movements, nothing to alarm or frighten the woman, who was already on edge.

Chloe watched his profile as he worked, noting the angle of his jaw, the blond stubble that covered it, the sharpness of his cheekbones, his flat, shell-shaped ears. She remembered how much she'd learnt from him when they'd worked together in Australia. His calmness, experience, patience and bedside manner were some of the many things that she'd found attractive but they hadn't been the first things she'd noticed about him. She hadn't even known he was a doctor, let alone that she'd be working with him, when she'd first seen him. It had been one of those moments you read about: their eyes had met across a room and she was done for. She'd fallen hard and fast.

She blinked and cleared her mind as she took a deep breath and told herself to focus. There were more important things to think about than what had happened between her and Xander. Those days were long gone. She was a different person now, no longer carefree, no longer independent. She had a job to do and other things to consider. She needed to get herself under control. She couldn't let her hormones unsettle her. She needed to take stock of the situation—even if she couldn't make sense of it yet.

She had to try to ignore the fact that Xander was kneeling just inches away from her. She had to resist the temptation to reach out and place her hand on the back of his neck. To feel the warmth of his skin under her fingers. She had to pretend he was just another colleague, not the man who she'd once thought could be the love of her life.

She forced her attention back to the tableau in front of her, concentrating on the woman's chest instead of on Xander.

He'd found the space he wanted and she watched as he inserted the needle between the woman's ribs. They all heard the air as it flowed out of the chest cavity. He removed the needle after a few seconds, leaving the plastic tube in situ, and reviewed the woman's observations. Her oxygen sats improved as her chest re-inflated. Xander listened for breath sounds before taking a chest seal from Rick and applying it.

Rick and Xander worked smoothly together, inserting a drip, administering pain relief and hooking an oxygen mask over Shania's nose and mouth while Xander kept up his explanations.

They didn't need Chloe's help but she kept

herself busy, finding the things she might need for a delivery and making sure they were close to hand. Focusing on anything but Xander.

'How are you feeling now, Shania?' Xander asked. 'Do you have any pain? Can you tell me where it is?'

'Ow!' Shania clutched at her stomach and Chloe could see the tell-tale ripple of a contraction pass across Shania's abdomen. Treating a tension pneumothorax always gave immediate relief and Xander had relieved Shania's chest pain so successfully that she was now complaining about her labour pains.

Xander caught Chloe's eye and gave her a quick smile, uniting them in their treatment of their patient. But his smile did more than that. Chloe thought he was handsome when he wore his usual brooding expression but when he smiled he was something else altogether. No longer wounded, or sad, the shadows in his eyes disappeared and it was like watching the sun come out after a long winter. His smile instantly transformed his face and made Chloe's world tilt. It had been almost four years since she'd seen his smile and it knocked the wind out of her all over again.

'Looks like it's your turn,' he said as he stood preparing to swap places with Chloe. Space was at a premium and Chloe was very aware of how close to her Xander was standing. How she had to brush past him in order to reach their patient.

She took a deep breath and mentally shook her head as she knelt on the floor.

'Shania, I'm Chloe. I'm a midwife. Let's see what's going on with this baby of yours, shall we?' She strapped a foetal heart rate monitor around Shania's belly and waited anxiously for the reading, hoping it would fall between one hundred and ten and one hundred and sixty beats per minute.

One hundred and two…

'We need to get her to hospital,' Chloe said. The baby appeared to be in distress and Chloe was concerned about oxygen deprivation given Shania's injuries.

'I'm not going to the hospital,' Shania protested.

'We need to transfer you,' Chloe insisted. 'You have a chest wound and you're having a baby. This is for your safety. And your baby's safety.'

'Who will look after my kids?' Shania asked as another contraction gripped her.

'Where are they?' Xander asked.

'With one of the neighbours.' A policewoman stood in the corner of the kitchen.

Chloe had barely been aware of her until she replied to Xander's question.

Xander looked over to her. 'Can you see if the neighbour is happy to keep them for a while?'

The policewoman nodded and left the room and Chloe indicated to Rick to follow her. She needed him to fetch the stretcher.

She bent her head and resumed her examination. 'Let me have a quick look to see how far along your labour is.' The contractions were less than a minute apart and Chloe was worried. She looked up at Xander. 'I don't think we're going anywhere right now. She's fully dilated.'

The baby's head was crowning. There was nothing Chloe could do now to slow down Shania's labour. This baby was coming whether they were ready or not.

'I want to push!' Shania cried out.

'Okay, Shania, ready when you are.' The pain relief Xander administered was enough to lightly sedate Shania, enough to calm her down but not enough to make her unable to push.

Shania bore down and Chloe eased the baby's head out. 'Well done, Shania. Take a breath now,' she said as she felt for the cord.

Everything seemed clear. 'Wait for the next contraction and I'll get you to push again.'

The baby came out in a slippery rush. A girl. She didn't appear to be injured but everything was silent. No crying and Chloe didn't think she was even breathing. She quickly wrapped her in a soft cloth and rubbed her vigorously and was rewarded with a muted cry.

'Congratulations, Shania. You have a daughter.'

Chloe clamped and cut the cord and did a quick Apgar assessment. The baby's hands and feet were blue, her respiration slow, but she scored an eight out of ten, which was great, all things considered.

Chloe wrapped her against the cold and slid a cap onto her head to retain warmth. 'Do you have a name for her?' she asked as she handed her to Shania.

'Tonya.' Shania was gazing at her daughter, all pain forgotten.

Shania was oblivious to her surroundings now as Chloe delivered the placenta and put it into a bag. Shania still needed to go to hospital and Chloe needed to take the placenta with them.

Rick returned with the stretcher followed by the policewoman. Chloe could see the surprised look on her face. The baby had arrived faster than anyone anticipated. The policewoman spoke to Shania. 'Shania, your neighbour will mind the children while you go to hospital.'

Shania was too tired to argue as Chloe took the baby and Rick and Xander transferred her to the stretcher.

Chloe did another quick check of the baby and increased her Apgar score by one. Despite the dramatic circumstances surrounding her birth she was doing remarkably well. Chloe carried Tonya out to the chopper and held her as Shania's stretcher was loaded on board and Rick connected Shania to the monitors. Simon lifted the chopper into the air as soon as Rick gave the all clear.

'The police asked me to let you know you'll need to make a report,' Xander said to Shania. 'They want to know if you want to press charges.'

Shania shook her head. 'I'm not going to press charges.'

Xander looked incredulous. 'What? Why not?'

'If I'm in hospital I need Greg at home to look after the other kids. I can't have him locked up overnight. They'll keep him until he sobers up and then they'll let him go. I just hope he goes home and not back to the pub.'

'The police have arrested Greg. I don't think they're going to be too quick to let him go.' Xander was speaking slowly, as if he was worried that Shania wasn't understanding the situation. 'Has he been physically violent towards you before?'

'I started it,' Shania replied, and Chloe noticed she avoided answering Xander's question.

'How do you figure that?'

'I was going to the next-door neighbour's. I was going to ask her to drive me to hospital because Greg had been drinking, but Greg got angry. He didn't want the neighbours to know he was in no state to drive and he insisted he was okay to take me. I knew he wasn't and when I tried to get past him he blocked my way. I grabbed a kitchen knife and threatened him but he took it off me and, when I tried to push past him, the knife stabbed into me. I shouldn't have taken the knife in the first place and then none of this would have happened.'

Chloe could see by Xander's expression that he wasn't pleased with Shania's answer. She also knew he wouldn't be pleased that there was nothing he could do about the situation.

She knew he was driven by the same over-whelming desire to help people, to fight for the underdog, to improve people's lives, as she was. 'Shania, the knife didn't stab you, your husband did. That is *not* okay.'

'Do you have kids?' Shania asked.

Chloe should have anticipated the question. It was one she got asked by almost every labouring mother when they were looking for some common ground or reassurance that Chloe knew what they were going through, but she hadn't been prepared to have to answer that question in front of Xander. Her heart rate spiked but thank God she didn't have to answer as fortunately Shania was addressing Xander and not her.

Xander shook his head. 'No, I don't.' He kept his head turned away and Chloe wasn't able to see his expression. When she'd last seen him four years ago he hadn't wanted kids. Had anything changed? Would he want Lily?

'I have three kids,' Shania continued. 'Four now. I don't work. Where would I go?'

Xander looked up and Chloe took over from him. She knew he'd be wanting to offer advice but she guessed he wasn't sure how the system worked in the UK.

'There are options,' Chloe said. 'I can organise for a social worker to come and see you and we can see what measures we can put in place.' It was often a difficult process. Resources were scant and Chloe knew that a lot of mums preferred not to uproot their children. It was a catch-22. She'd start with getting the social worker visit while Shania was in hospital but she knew from experience that there was little they could do if Shania wasn't on board with the idea. She was sure Shania had heard it all before but she was pleased to see her give a very slight nod of agreement just as the large red *H* of the hospital helipad came into view beneath them.

The hospital roof became a hive of activity as the helicopter door slid open. Surgical and neonatal teams were on hand to meet them and transfer the patients and Chloe lost sight of Xander as she went with baby Tonya to the neonatal unit.

Her hands shook as she transferred Tonya to the neonatal stretcher. Her heart rate was still elevated and she knew some of it was due to adrenalin from the job but the rest was wholly and solely because of Xander.

She remained on tenterhooks for the rest of her shift waiting to see if Xander would appear in A&E even though she knew his shift must have finished well before hers. The air ambulance helicopter only operated during daylight hours and it was long since dark. Once the helicopter was out of action, road crews took over and Xander would have gone home. The only reason he would have to come to A&E would be to see her.

She was partly relieved and partly disappointed when her shift ended with Xander nowhere in sight.

Xander sat at the bar and nursed his drink as he mulled over the day's turn of events.

He wasn't thinking about work or Shania. He was thinking about Chloe. Seeing her had completely blindsided him and had brought back memories he'd thought long buried.

He hadn't let himself consider the possibility of seeing her again even though he was in London. But was it really such a surprise?

They'd met when she was on a study exchange, working with the flying doctor, and he knew that the London air ambulance was the UK equivalent but he'd had no idea she was working with them. He hadn't let himself hope that he'd see her again.

But here she was.

It had been almost four years but she'd barely changed. Maybe she wasn't quite as thin but, if anything, the few extra pounds suited her. She still looked young—she was seven years younger than him so she must only be about twenty-seven—but there was a maturity about her now. In both looks and manner. He saw it in her eyes and he'd seen it in her work today. She'd been confident, assured and capable.

He closed his eyes as he pictured her.

Her thick blond curls had been pulled back into a ponytail today, but he could remember how it had felt to slide his fingers into her tresses, how her hair had felt splayed across his bare chest. How she'd felt lying nestled into his side, how he had felt when she'd taken him in her arms. The cool, silkiness of her skin, the softness of her lips and the smell of shampoo and sun in her hair. He recalled it all.

It had been almost four years but he remembered her as if it was yesterday.

She had been a good distraction, an *excellent* distraction, at a time of his life when he'd needed distracting.

He'd had a tumultuous two years and he had still been trying to process what had happened when she walked into his life. He'd encountered two of life's major stresses simultaneously. A serious health scare and a marriage breakdown. His cancer diagnosis had been a shock, his wife's infidelity equally so. Going through chemotherapy had been confronting and exhausting without the additional stress of a divorce. A divorce that he hadn't seen coming. Those past two years had left him shattered and numb and he had been struggling to find his new identity in a future that didn't hold marriage or fatherhood. His dreams had been crushed, leaving him with nothing except his career.

He had been physically and emotionally exhausted when he'd met Chloe. He'd been through the wringer and, although he knew a stranger would look at him and suspect nothing, he felt a shadow of his former self.

She'd made him feel better but she hadn't been able to mend him.

Chloe had given him a chance to forget about the previous two years. Some respite. She'd allowed him a chance to ignore what had happened but, he could admit this now, that hadn't helped him to deal with it. Denial and acceptance were two completely different things.

But he did know that the last time he'd been truly happy had been when he'd been with Chloe. She had calmed his soul and brought peace and happiness to his life at a time when he'd desperately needed it. And then taken it all away with her again when she'd left.

He hadn't anticipated that her departure would leave such a big hole in his life—after all, they'd only known each other for four weeks—but the loneliness he felt had surprised him and it was only after she'd gone that he wondered if he should have confided in her. Could they have had something more if he hadn't been so emotionally wounded? So damaged.

He would never know.

Confiding in her would have meant talking about what had happened, talking about his feelings, and he wasn't ready to do that. He was happier in denial. They'd shared a bed but not their minds. His wife, ex-wife, whom he'd known for ten years, had betrayed his trust and he hadn't been in a position where he could bring himself to trust anyone else with his story. Not even a virtual stranger.

He'd needed time.

And time was something they didn't have then.

He may have denied them the opportunity of getting to know each other better but he consoled himself with the knowledge that Chloe was only ever in Australia temporarily. He told himself that nothing he could have said or done would have changed that but it didn't stop him from sometimes wishing that things had turned out differently.

They'd had no plans for a future together, although he had found himself imagining one, but he knew he wasn't in a position to offer her anything permanent. The future. Permanency. They were words that he'd been afraid to consider. His fate was still uncertain. He'd enjoyed Chloe's company but he'd known, in his soul, that he wasn't what she needed even while he thought she might be exactly what he desired.

But he had to sort himself out first. He had to find some level of acceptance for what had happened to him. To his life. He couldn't move forward until he'd done that.

He didn't know what his future was going to be, so instead of searching for her he'd gone searching the world, looking for a substitute. Looking for something to fill the space she'd left behind.

He'd thought he would find something to fill that void but today, seeing her again, he wondered whether his search had been in vain. Could anything fill that void or could it only be filled by someone?

She'd been the perfect tonic for him at one of the lowest points of his life but what about now?

Was he in a better place?

Four years on and he'd thought he was better but his feelings today took him by surprise. He'd felt an extraordinary sense of calm when he'd seen her today. As if, for the first time in years, he could breathe deeply and fully.

He'd considered asking her out for a coffee or a drink but had hesitated at the last minute. He needed some time to understand what this chance meeting could mean. Was it just that? A chance. It didn't need to mean anything. He didn't need to act on it. He needed time to digest this situation. To figure it out.

Being in the same place again was just a coincidence and he didn't believe in coincidences.

But he couldn't deny that it had been good to see her again.

He swallowed a mouthful of beer as he recalled the first time he'd laid eyes on her.

He'd been sitting by himself at the bar in the Palace Hotel in Broken Hill—some things never changed, he thought wryly, although he had been waiting for a colleague. He'd been drinking too much, blocking out the previous two years. He'd already had one beer and was on to his second when she walked in.

The late-afternoon sun had silhouetted her in the doorway of the hotel and her golden curls had shone like a halo around her head.

She was slim and elegant with a dancer's posture and a graceful walk.

He'd sat, mesmerised, as she'd walked towards him. He hadn't stopped to wonder why she was heading his way; at the time it had made perfect sense, as if his mind was willing her to come to him, as if she could read his thoughts. It was only when she joined him at the bar that he noticed that Jane, a Royal Flying Doctor flight nurse and one of his colleagues, was with her.

Jane introduced them and the news that this vision, Chloe, was going to be working with him for the next month was the best thing he'd heard in a long, long time. From that moment on he was scarcely aware of other colleagues and patrons coming and going around them. He was struck, not only by Chloe's natural beauty but by the joy that seemed to radiate from her. He'd been enthralled by her smile, her lips, the light in her brown eyes and her exuberance.

He had no idea of how long they'd stayed in the bar. All he knew was that he wasn't leaving until she did and eventually it was just the two of them, alone. One by one the others had left but Chloe had stayed on and, therefore, so had he.

She didn't have anywhere she had to be.

She'd flirted with him. Touched him on the arm. The thigh. Playing with her glorious hair. He thought he was too old for her, he was about to turn thirty but he'd felt ten years more than that; he *was* old but not so old that he didn't recognise the signs of mutual attraction.

He'd wondered, briefly, if it was a bad idea to let her know he was interested too but he hadn't wanted to resist. Hadn't been able to. Chloe had been very convincing and he hadn't fought against her for too long. He had behaved for one night but they both knew what was going to happen.

He remembered the anticipation.

Being with Chloe was the first thing he'd looked forward to for months.

He had been working with the Royal Flying Doctor Service for six months. It had long been a dream of his that had been squashed by his ex-wife, but when he'd finally made it to the service he'd felt a sense of relief that he was starting to put the past behind him rather than the sense of excitement he'd always hoped for. Chloe turned out to be the first bit of excitement he'd had in a long time. They'd had a brief but passionate affair. His head wasn't in the right place for anything more and she was only in town for a month, but it had been a bright point in an otherwise dark period of his life.

Their affair had burned bright. Their chemistry overshadowing conversation. Chloe was young, carefree, on a working holiday; she wasn't interested in anything deep and meaningful. He was jaded; he didn't want to dampen her enthusiasm for life with his tales of woe. That wasn't what she needed. It wasn't what *he* needed. He wanted to forget about his troubles and she allowed him to do that.

She was addictive.

Restorative.

And then she was gone.

CHAPTER THREE

CHLOE FOLDED HERSELF into a seat on the Tube. She was tired—it had been a long day and a busy shift—but her mind was buzzing. Memories of Xander, snippets of the past, filled her thoughts.

The subway tiles whizzed past as the train zipped through the stations. The press of bodies, the fluorescent lighting and the blackness of the tunnels suffocated her. She closed her eyes against the glare of the lights and let her mind drift back to four years ago.

The London Underground couldn't be further from the Australian outback. The close confines of the flying doctor plane had been replaced by the trains on the underground and the occasional helicopter flight. Going to the pub in Broken Hill or the races had been replaced with an occasional girls' night out and trips to the park with Lily. The feel of the sunlight on her skin and the smell of the eucalyptus trees and dirt had been replaced with the hospital air-conditioning and the polluted air of London.

Even in the outback there had never been complete darkness but instead of artificial lighting it had been the stars overhead. Instead of the press of bodies sometimes it was just her, Xander, the pilot and a patient. Four people in thousands of square kilometres.

Sometimes it had just been her and Xander under the night sky.

It had been such a short period in her life but she'd never forgotten it. How could she?

Her mind drifted back to the night she'd met Xander. To the night that changed her life.

She had just arrived in Broken Hill, in the Australian outback. It was her third and final month on a study exchange program with the flying doctor service. She'd already completed stints in Adelaide and Port Augusta and had loved every minute of it but she was hugely excited about being in the real outback. Broken Hill was what she'd pictured when she'd applied for the exchange. It was so totally different to anything she would ever experience back home and she couldn't wait.

Jane, one of the flight nurses, had taken her to drinks at the Palace Hotel. It was tradition for any newcomers to the service. The imposing two-storey redbrick hotel with its unusual internal artwork—murals that covered not only the walls but the ceilings too—had featured in several popular Australian movies and Chloe had been keen to visit the iconic hotel. But when they'd walked into the bar her attention had been captured, not by the architecture or artwork, but by a man sitting alone at the bar.

She couldn't remember anything else.

Tall, blond, long, lean and tanned. He was physically perfect. In Chloe's opinion he had not even one flaw.

He was wearing pale cotton trousers that moulded to his backside and a dark T-shirt that clung to his chest and showed off muscular arms. Every blond hair on his head was perfectly in place.

His skin was flawless, not a freckle to distract attention. His nose was straight, his jaw square, his shoulders broad. His eyebrows, a slightly darker blond than his hair, framed a pair of grey eyes. Physically he was perfect but there was something wounded in his expression. Something lost in his grey eyes. He cut a solitary, lonely figure and Chloe couldn't resist.

She'd always been drawn to the damaged, the wounded. She had seen the pain her father's treatment of her mother had caused. It had affected Chloe and her brothers too, and as the eldest child she had always felt a responsibility and desire to try to fix things for everyone. She wanted to make the world a better, happier place and she'd been fascinated by the solitary man at the bar, by his sense of loneliness and touch of despair. She'd been immediately interested and desperate to know more.

She couldn't remember whether Jane had led her to him or if she'd made a beeline herself. Either way, it didn't matter. She'd been captivated. She'd stayed long after Jane and the other flying doctor personnel had left. Talking to Xander.

She'd known instinctively that she would sleep with him. It wasn't a case of 'if' but 'when.'

It had been an amazing four weeks, a magical month, a pocket of time that she'd expected she would wrap up in her bank of memories. Something to be taken out and relived when she needed something to smile about. She hadn't expected to relive it every time she looked into her daughter's eyes.

But despite the way things had turned out she wouldn't change anything. Well, maybe a few things. It had been a simple time in her life with no one to think about except for herself. That had certainly changed and she wouldn't go back to a time before Lily but that didn't mean there wasn't something to be said for an uncomplicated life.

Unfortunately, she felt in her bones that her life was about to become decidedly *more* complicated with Xander's unexpected appearance. And she needed time to work out what she was going to do about it.

'That's enough riding for now, Lily, why don't you go on the slide.' Chloe felt like a bad mother, cutting short Lily's ride on her new bike, but she was tired; she'd slept badly, and she needed a break from running after Lily to give her a little push every time she needed to restart her bike.

'Is everything all right?' her mother asked as Chloe wheeled the bike back to the park bench and Lily scampered off to the slide. 'You look tired.'

'I didn't sleep well,' Chloe admitted to her mother.

'Problems at work?' Susan was a nurse too; she was familiar with the pitfalls of the job, with those days that you couldn't leave behind at the hospital, with those patients who continued to live in your head even once your shift was finished.

'Sort of. We have a new doctor at the air ambulance.'

A doctor whose arrival meant that Chloe had tossed and turned all night but still hadn't been able to figure out what she was going to do about him.

'Was he or she difficult to work with?'

'No.' She needed her mother's advice. 'It's Xander.'

'Your Xander?'

Chloe nodded. Her mother and Chloe's brothers were the only people who knew about him. 'He's not mine, but yes.'

'What is he doing here?'

'He's covering sick leave. He's only here for a few weeks.'

'So you think it's just a coincidence?'

'What?'

'That he's turned up here, working with the Air Ambulance Service?'

'It must be.' Chloe didn't believe in coincidences—she always thought things happened for a reason—but it had to be. He couldn't have come looking for her. She had only started working at the Queen Victoria Hospital after coming home from Australia. She'd applied to work there because it was the base for the Air Ambulance Service but Xander couldn't know that.

'Does he know about Lily?'

Chloe shook her head. 'How could he?' Chloe hadn't even put his name on Lily's birth certificate. She hadn't been able to without his consent.

'What are you going to do?'

'I'll have to tell him. I looked for him for six months.' She'd only stopped when Lily had been born—time and money had made it impractical to keep searching for someone who seemed to have completely disappeared. 'I just don't know when. That's why I'm tired. I've been awake all night thinking about what to do.'

Chloe had long since accepted that she would raise Lily as a single mother. Perhaps it wasn't ideal but it wasn't impossible and she was managing. What effect would Xander's reappearance have?

'It's been four years. How do you think he'll react to the news?' she asked her mother.

'I have no way of knowing. Some men will rise to the challenge, others may not—every one is different and so is every situation—and unfortunately, he's disappeared once before. But there's only one way to know for sure.'

Chloe sighed. 'He has never looked for me. He must have been happy to let me go.'

Her mother raised an eyebrow. 'You don't know that. And that doesn't mean he won't want to be a father. That's two very different relationships.'

'I don't think they're that easy to separate. My father couldn't do it.'

'Your father left me but he never intended to leave you children. Our marriage was over—his actions damaged it irreparably—but he didn't abandon you. He wasn't planning on dying.' Her mother looked over to where Lily slid happily down the slide. 'You owe it to Lily to tell Xander about her. You owe it to him too. There probably isn't going to be the perfect time. You're probably better off just getting it out in the open.'

'No.' Chloe shook her head. 'I need to find out more. I need to know why he's here. What's been going on in his life? What if he has a family of his own? He might not thank me for disrupting his life.'

She wondered if he'd changed that much. If he'd finally decided he wanted children. Or if he was still convinced he didn't. He might not want to know about Lily. Or worse, he might want Lily but not Chloe. 'There are far too many questions and you know how I hate asking a question that I don't know the answer to.'

Chloe didn't believe in coincidences and she didn't like surprises. She needed to collect the facts before she started disseminating information that could change everyone's lives.

She didn't really know him. She didn't know how he would react to this news. She hadn't known four years ago and she was no wiser now. The truth was, after Lily was born and she'd come to terms with the fact that Xander was gone, a part of her had been secretly relived that she hadn't been able to find him. It meant she didn't have to deal with any unpleasantness. Fantasy and reality were rarely the same thing.

She still needed to find out why he was here. What did his arrival mean for her? And for Lily?

Did he have a family? He wasn't wearing a wedding ring. What were his thoughts on fatherhood and commitment now? Four years was a long time. Things may have changed but she didn't want to tell him about Lily if he wasn't going to love her. Life was hard enough without being unloved or unwanted. She wouldn't expose her daughter to that.

'I think you're making excuses,' her mother told her.

Chloe knew she was but she was scared.

She knew she had to tell him about Lily, but when?

And what if someone else told him first? Shania had almost asked the question and her air ambulance colleagues knew she had a daughter. They never had a lot of time to chat about their personal lives when they were on a job; the flights were never more than eleven minutes in duration and they were either preparing for a job or often caring for a patient on a return. It wasn't often that they came back empty-handed. But what if one of her colleagues said something?

Thank God she wouldn't have to spend hours with Xander. Not that she'd minded four years ago but until she worked out what she was going to do about the situation she was better off keeping her distance. Luckily, she didn't spend her days in the air ambulance unit waiting for a call; she was only ever an additional team member, called in specially for certain jobs.

Her mother gave her a hug. 'There's only one way to know how this will turn out, Chloe, and that's to tell him the truth. You'll soon find out what he thinks then.'

Her mind and the discussion went around in a never-ending circle and by the time Lily got bored with the playground Chloe was no closer to a decision about what to do. No closer to figuring out how to deal with Xander's unexpected appearance.

Xander was edgy. It was a busy shift, most of them were. On average the air ambulance attended five call-outs each day but it wasn't the caseload that had him unsettled. Each time they received a call he was on tenterhooks, waiting to see if they would need a midwife, waiting to find out if he would see Chloe. He felt like he'd thought of nothing and no one but her for the past three days and he was determined to ask her out next time he saw her. Nothing ventured, nothing gained. But at the end of his shift he knew he couldn't continue just to wait for fate, or an emergency, to intervene. He was going quietly crazy. He'd have to go and find her.

He changed out of his orange flight overalls and headed down to A&E only to be told she was up in the maternity wards.

As he stepped out of the lift Chloe's golden curls caught his eye. Her back was to him as she pushed a wheelchair down the corridor. He could see she had a patient with her and he waited to see where she was going. He didn't want to have this conversation in public. She stopped at the door to the NICU, swiping her card and letting herself in. It was only a minute or so before she reappeared, by which time he was walking casually towards her.

'Xander! What are you doing here?'

'I thought I'd drop past and see how Shania was doing,' he said, improvising quickly to explain his presence.

'Physically she's doing well and she also had an interview with a social worker. She hasn't made any major decisions yet but at least she's looking at her options.'

'And the baby? Tonya?'

'She's doing brilliantly too. I've just taken Shania to the NICU to see her. They're both doing well.'

'In that case I won't interrupt,' he said as he fell into step beside her. 'Have you finished your shift?'

'No, not quite. Why?' she asked as she pressed the button to call the lift.

'I wondered if you'd like to have a drink with me? Tonight, after work?'

'Why?'

He hadn't expected her to question his reasons. 'To catch up,' he said simply. 'I wasn't expecting to see you. It was a nice surprise and I'd like to hear about what you've been up to.'

'I can't.'

'You can't tonight or can't full stop?' he asked as Chloe's phone buzzed in her pocket.

She took her phone out and looked at the screen as the lift arrived and the doors slid open. She stepped into the lift and turned to face him. She said, 'I'm sorry. I need to go,' but didn't answer his question.

The lift doors closed, leaving him standing in the corridor. Alone.

He was an idiot. Just because he was still single, confused by his feelings and out of his depth, didn't mean she was still in the same position. Of course she'd be busy. She had a life. He'd noticed she didn't wear a wedding ring but that didn't mean she didn't have a significant other. It had been four years.

Four years ago she'd brought light back into his life and he'd been searching for it again ever since. But that didn't mean she felt the same way. They'd had undeniable chemistry but that didn't mean to say she hadn't found that with somebody else.

He should leave her alone. He was old enough to know one shouldn't go back. But he didn't want to give up. Not yet.

He'd given her up once before.

* * *

Chloe tried to resist the temptation to look at her watch. Again. She couldn't believe she'd agreed to let Esther set her up on a date with one of Harry's friends. She had hoped that the date would help keep her mind off Xander's reappearance but it wasn't working.

She tried to be a bit more engaging. It wasn't Stephen's fault she wasn't giving this date her full attention. He was pleasant enough but he wasn't the one she wanted to spend an evening with. She should have cancelled the date or at least rescheduled—she knew she was wasting his time and hers—but it was too late now. She found herself constantly comparing Stephen to Xander and he was falling short.

She knew it wasn't Stephen per se. In the past four years no one had given her the same feeling of excitement and anticipation that she'd experienced with Xander and she was worried that her four weeks with Xander had ruined her chances of finding someone else whom she could fall in love with.

Her thoughts drifted as Stephen tried gamely to engage her in conversation. She wondered what Xander was doing right now. She'd had to turn down his invitation, not only because she'd already agreed to this date but because she hadn't worked out what to tell him. She'd panicked when he invited her out. Her first thought had been, *Did he know about Lily? Was that what he'd wanted to talk to her about?* And despite telling herself there was no way he could know anything she'd gradually worked herself into a state.

She'd hoped her date with Stephen would be a good distraction, would give her something else to think about other than Xander, but it was *not* going well. If she was honest, it was a disaster. She wondered at what point it wouldn't be considered rude to make her excuses and leave.

'Harry said you work with him at the Queen Victoria. You're a nurse?'

'A midwife. In A&E.' Chloe made a concerted effort to tune back into the conversation. 'I work with the air ambulance service too,' she added. Most people found that aspect of her job interesting. Maybe Stephen would ask enough questions that she could focus on that.

'How did you get into that?' he asked, almost on cue.

'I spent some time in Australia on a study exchange working with their flying doctor service. I loved it so much that I applied for the air ambulance when I got back. It's the closest thing we have.'

'And what did you think of Australia?'

'I loved it. Have you been there?'

He nodded. 'I spent twelve months there as a Fellow. Couldn't stand it. The heat was terrible and those awful flies, not to mention the endless discussions about sport.'

Chloe had loved her time in Australia. Not the flies—she'd have to agree with him on that—but she'd loved everything else. She'd loved the relaxed lifestyle. She'd loved the weather. She'd loved the people. She'd loved Xander.

She sighed. Other than their careers as medical professionals she knew she and Stephen had nothing else in common and she figured there was absolutely no point in wasting any more of the evening for either of them. Thank God she hadn't agreed to dinner.

She excused herself from the table. She'd go to the ladies' and call her mum. She'd get her to text and say Lily was running a temperature and needed her. She knew a normal person would see that for the excuse it was but she didn't care. She'd be doing both of them a favour by cutting the night short.

Chloe slipped her phone back into her bag as she left the toilets and returned to the table telling herself she could manage another five minutes until her mum called with a reprieve.

She had taken two steps in that direction when she heard her name.

'Chloe!'

She closed her handbag and looked up into a pair of familiar grey eyes.

Xander.

She stopped in her tracks, incapable of moving. She could feel her heart racing in her chest and wondered if he could see it beating beneath her shirt.

Why was he here? Was he meeting someone? Had he invited someone else for a drink when she'd turned him down or was this just a coincidence?

'What are you doing here?' he continued. 'Did you change your mind about that drink?'

Chloe shook her head. 'No. I'm on a date.'

'Oh. Of course.'

Chloe tried to read his expression, to decipher his tone. Was he disappointed? And what did he mean by 'of course'? She hardly ever went on dates; this was the first one this year, the second one in four months. But she couldn't explain her reluctance to date and the reason why her opportunities were limited without divulging her secret. Or should that be secrets, plural? That no one measured up to her memory of him and that she was a single mother.

'Are you meeting someone here?' she asked.

'No.'

Was his presence here just a coincidence?

'It's good to see you but don't let me keep you,' he said, leaving her free to go.

Maybe she would have to start believing in coincidences, she thought as she reluctantly returned to her table and her date.

If she could get rid of Stephen perhaps she could salvage her evening?

He watched her walk away before taking a seat at the bar.

What was it about Chloe? he thought as he nodded to the barman and held up one finger, indicating his usual, as he took a seat. He was a sensible, intelligent man but whenever he saw her, whenever she was near, all logical thoughts seemed to evaporate. Of course, she wouldn't have known he would be at that pub. It was close to the Queen Victoria Hospital but it wasn't the closest and it wasn't the local for the hospital staff. It was, however, near the short-term rental apartment where he was staying and he'd got into the habit of stopping in for a beer and something to eat. It was simpler to be fed than to cook and it gave him some company.

He'd just swallowed the first mouthful of his beer when Chloe reappeared.

'Is this seat taken?'

She was smiling and his heart leapt. Had she ditched her date? For him? He couldn't help the feeling of excitement as she sat on the bar stool next to him. The anticipation was familiar. *She* was familiar.

'What happened to your date?'

'He left.'

'What?'

She laughed and the sound was so familiar, so comforting, that it lifted his spirits even when he hadn't realised his spirits needing lifting. He hadn't realised a lot of things. Once again, Chloe brought light into his life, only this time he hadn't been aware of the darkness. Four years ago he'd known he was in a dark place and Chloe had got him out of it. He slipped back after she'd left and despite his concerted efforts to find happiness and make peace with the world he knew now he hadn't been successful.

'I told him that it wasn't working for me and I didn't want to waste more of his time.'

'Are you leaving too?'

'No,' she replied as she shook her head. Her

bright golden curls glowed in the light as she shook her head. She was striking, vivacious, a beacon.

'Good. Will you have that drink with me now?'

'Are you sure you're not meeting friends?'

'No.' He had a few friends in London—acquaintances, really, all in the medical field—but most were now married with children and they didn't have the flexibility or luxury of being able to meet for a mid-week dinner. He'd caught up with a few for a drink or two on occasion but, ultimately, they all had to go home to their wives and families. 'And even if I was, you'd still be welcome to join us. But I'm here because I'm staying just around the corner. I'm just grabbing some dinner and a beer,' he said as the barman handed him a wooden board with a burger and a side of fries on it. 'Have you eaten?'

'No. I'm not hungry but I'll stay for a drink.'

'A gin and tonic?'

'Yes. Thank you,' she said as she reached over and pinched a chip off his plate. That was familiar too. He remembered she would order own her meal and then prefer to eat his.

'So the date went badly.'

'It wasn't the worst one I've ever had but it was close.' She was grinning. She didn't look

too upset. In fact, she didn't look upset at all—
she looked amazing.

'What seemed to be the problem?'

'He wasn't my type.'

'You have a type?'

'I guess so.'

The barman served Chloe's gin, placing it
on the bar. She couldn't believe Xander had
remembered her favourite drink and the idea
that he had pleased her. She was glad she'd
come back to find him after making her excuses to Stephen. She'd put Lily to bed before
heading out and her mum wasn't expecting
her home anytime soon. She had plenty of
time to have one drink with Xander. Just to
catch up on what he'd been doing.

He picked up her drink and put it in front of
her. His leg brushed against hers and the contact made her jump. It was nothing, really—
his knee brushed the outside of her thigh—but
she could feel his body heat even through her
trousers and her body responded to his touch.

'So, your type,' he said as she stirred her
drink, 'describe him to me.'

She took a sip of her drink, taking a moment to gather her thoughts. 'Someone with
a bit more energy. Someone who makes me
feel excited. Filled with possibility. Someone
who makes me wonder what happens next.'

Someone who made her feel like Xander did.

'You're talking about chemistry,' he said.

She nodded and put her glass back on the bar and tried to ignore the fact that his leg was still resting against hers.

Sitting at the bar with Xander felt the same but different.

Familiar but strange.

Things had changed. At least for Chloe. She was no longer young and carefree. She was a single mother with responsibilities. But the chemistry was still there. She was still drawn to him. She longed to touch him properly, to see if her memories were real.

He was still gorgeous. Still a Norse god. His grey eyes still held a trace of melancholy. She'd always attributed that to his divorce but surely that couldn't still be the case. He'd been divorced almost five years now. He must have put that behind him?

She forced herself to focus on the present. She couldn't dwell in the past.

'How long have you been living in Wales?' she asked when she recovered her power of speech. She was desperate to know where he'd been and what he'd been doing for the past four years but she couldn't ask such a direct question.

He frowned, his grey eyes cloudy. 'I don't live in Wales.'

'Oh, I thought Rick said you had come down from Wales to cover Eloise's sick leave.'

'I've been working in Wales with their air ambulance unit but it wasn't permanent. It was a six-month rotation. I was glad to get out of there, to be honest. I didn't mind Wales but it wasn't the smartest move, spending winter there. I should have timed it better.'

'And what are your plans when you finish with us?' she asked. She needed to find out where he was going next. Did she need to tell him about Lily if he had no plans to stay in England? Was there any point in disrupting everyone's lives? She and Lily were fine—they'd been fine for years on their own. They didn't need Xander and he might not need them.

He might not *want* them.

He might not want her.

The drink he had bought her could be for old times' sake. He wasn't wearing a wedding ring but that didn't mean he didn't have a wife or significant other waiting for him somewhere.

'I haven't worked it out yet.'

'Are you travelling with family?' she asked as the barman cleared the remnants of Xander's dinner away.

'No. We're both still single. What are the chances?'

'Coincidence?' she said with a smile.

'I don't believe in coincidences.'

'Me either.'

He was holding her gaze and she was lost. She couldn't think. She could only feel.

He reached for her and the clocks stopped.

He tucked a stray curl behind her ear and Chloe's knees trembled. 'It's been a long time,' he said as she held her breath. 'It's good to see you. Did I mention I'm staying just around the corner?'

The invitation was unspoken but there was no mistaking it. But she couldn't accept. She had to get home. To her daughter. Their daughter.

'You did.'

'Would you like to come back for a coffee?'

Chloe smiled. 'You know I don't drink coffee at night.' She wondered if he remembered that too.

'I do.'

Her smile got wider. 'Will you take a rain check? I'm on an early tomorrow.'

'I will.'

She slid off the bar stool and picked up her coat. She needed to get out of here while she still could. Before she made a hasty, hormonal decision that she would more than likely regret when her head overtook her heart again.

'I'll walk you out to a cab.'

'It's okay, I'm taking the Tube.'

Xander shook his head. 'No, it's late. That doesn't sound safe.'

'I do it all the time after work.'

'Really?'

She nodded as he held the door for her.

She stopped on the footpath, reluctant to walk away but knowing she had to go. A cab pulled up on the street beside them.

'Please, let me pay for a cab,' Xander offered. 'I'll feel better.' He reached out and opened the door, ensuring the cabbie couldn't drive away, but then he took her hand, holding her back before she could step inside.

She turned to him. Instinctively. Her breath caught in her throat as he stroked the palm of her hand with his thumb. She was pinned by the force of his grey eyes. Held immobile by the intensity of his gaze. She couldn't breathe. The air was thick with tension. Her mouth was dry, her skin warm, her cheeks flushed. Her heart was beating quickly and her stomach was fluttering.

'Are you sure you have to go?'

She nodded.

He bent his head until his mouth was next to her ear. His breath was warm on her cheek as he repeated her earlier words back to her.

'Are you sure you don't want to find out what happens next?'

She knew what was coming and she was powerless to resist. She didn't want to resist. She turned her face towards him and whispered, 'I know what happens next.' And then his lips were on hers. Warm, soft. Then harder.

She parted her lips and tasted him. He tasted familiar. He tasted sweet.

Her body remembered his touch. Her skin remembered the softness of his mouth. Her tongue remembered his taste.

The years fell away as the memory of him returned.

Xander's fingers were on her face, on her bare arms. Her skin was on fire and she melted against him as her body responded to his touch. She was aware of nothing else except the sensation of being fully alive. She wanted for nothing except Xander.

One hand was pressed to her spine, holding her close, and she could feel the heat of his palm through the thin fabric of her shirt. She felt her nipples harden as she pressed herself against his chest instead as she kissed him back. All her senses came to life and a line of fire spread from her stomach to her groin. She deepened the kiss, wanting to lose herself in Xander.

'Do you want the cab or not?'

She jumped as the cab driver's voice interrupted their moment. Her eyes flew open as Xander straightened up. He was studying her face as if committing each of her features to memory.

He smiled as his fingers trailed down the side of her cheek, sending a shiver of desire through her. Her heart was racing in her chest and her breaths were shallow.

'Are you sure you don't want to come back to my apartment?'

She hesitated. The kiss was wonderful. Magical. She felt as if time had stood still and brought her back to Xander, back into his arms, but she couldn't stay with him. She had responsibilities.

'I can't,' she said as she stepped back, breaking their connection. 'You promised me a rain check, remember?'

She waited for him to agree before she made herself get into the taxi. Made herself leave him.

He closed the door and blew her a kiss.

Chloe gave the driver her address but scarcely recalled getting home. Her world suddenly felt full of possibility but she needed to be sensible. She needed to be careful not to get carried away.

CHAPTER FOUR

CHLOE JOGGED ACROSS the helipad. This time she could see Xander's familiar figure in the chopper. She was looking for him and her heart rate increased. The memory of his kiss was still fresh in her mind. She could almost feel the imprint of his lips on hers still.

She smiled in greeting as she climbed aboard. Was it only a few days ago that he'd re-entered her life? She felt lighter. Happier. Full of hope.

Since he kissed her some of her doubts had vanished. She knew she was being fanciful; just because he made her toes tingle and her pulse race didn't mean he'd want to be a part of her life. It didn't mean he'd want to be a father but she couldn't help the lifting of her spirits. It was amazing what a good kiss had done for her frame of mind. The dark clouds had lightened a little.

She was remembering how she'd felt all

those years ago. How *he* made her feel. It was a long time since she'd been kissed senseless. Since she'd felt as if she could lose control.

But she needed to be careful. Last time she lost control she wound up pregnant.

But that thought still couldn't wipe the smile from her face as she fastened her harness and strapped herself into her seat as she listened to the situation report.

He smiled back at her and she imagined the shadows in his eyes had eased a little.

She blushed and looked away, focusing on the information being dispersed.

'We're attending a two-car MVA,' Rick said. 'Paramedics and fire service are at the scene. There are four patients. Two victims trapped and unconscious, a third with minor injuries and a fourth is a pregnant woman, thirty-six weeks' gestation, in cardiac arrest. Paramedics are giving ALS.'

Chloe translated the report in her head. Four victims of a motor vehicle accident: two status unknown, one conscious and mobile, one in a critical condition receiving advanced life support.

'We'll need to triage on arrival,' Xander instructed. He was back to business.

Chloe knew the order of treatment would be determined by a few things. Whether or not the fire crew had managed to extricate the trapped victims and what injuries they had sustained. Whether or not the paramedics had managed to resuscitate the woman and, if they hadn't, were they still trying or was she deceased. There were a lot of unknowns but this wasn't unusual. The job this time though was complicated by the number of victims. They'd been told four but, in Chloe's head, she was counting five. At thirty-six weeks' gestation the baby was potentially a fifth casualty.

Nine minutes after take-off Simon banked the helicopter over the M25. Beneath them Chloe could see the accident site on one of the approach roads. Flashing lights of the emergency vehicles lit up the grey and drizzly day and bounced off the reflective panels on the uniforms of the emergency teams. Debris was strewn across the road and she could see the fire service still working on one of the crumpled cars, trying to free the victims.

Police had cordoned off the road and Simon brought the chopper down on the bitumen as Chloe pulled on a pair of gloves. Rick had the door open as soon as they touched down and Chloe, Rick and Xander grabbed their kits and sprinted to the scene.

A woman lay on a spinal board on a stretcher, two paramedics in attendance. Between them Chloe could see the mound of her pregnancy. The woman had been intubated and was being manually ventilated by one of the paramedics.

A pair of ambulances had stopped on the hard shoulder. In the back of one sat an older woman. She had a blanket wrapped around her shoulders as a third paramedic cleaned her head wound. Chloe wondered if she was related to the pregnant woman. Someone must have given the first responders some background information.

Xander paused beside the stretcher and Chloe heard him introduce himself.

'What's the situation?'

'Thirty-year-old woman, thirty-six weeks' gestation, suffered a cardiac arrest, non-responsive. I've administered three milligrams of atropine and eight milligrams of epinephrine via IV. Intubated on the first attempt and manual ventilation continuing. She has a head trauma, most likely the cause of the cardiac arrest, a facial cyanosis and an abdominal seat-belt hematoma. I'm concerned about an abdominal haemorrhage.'

'We can do an abdominal ultrasound on board the chopper if she can be moved.'

The paramedics nodded and the woman was transferred to the helicopter. It took all of the first responders working in unison. Four to lift the spinal board while Chloe held the drip.

Xander cut through the woman's clothing while resuscitation attempts continued around him. Her exposed belly was tight and drum-like. Chloe had the ultrasound ready. She handed Xander the transducer and squeezed the aqueous gel onto the patient's abdomen.

There was a heartbeat but it belonged to the foetus.

'There are signs of an abdominal haemorrhage but the bleeding has slowed.'

'How long since ALS commenced?' Xander asked as he wiped off the ultrasound gel.

'Fourteen minutes.'

'And the delay between the cardiac arrest and treatment?'

'Several minutes.'

'We could lose them both at this rate.' Xander looked at Chloe. 'Do we try to save one?'

She knew he was talking about saving the baby.

She nodded.

'What are you going to do?' Rick asked.

'If you can continue ventilation, we can perform a C-section to deliver the baby.'

'Here?'

It was Xander's turn to nod.

'Have you done this before?'

'Once.'

Xander's grey eyes were dark. Chloe suspected from his expression that the last time didn't go so well. She hoped he'd learnt from the experience.

'Are you okay to help me?' he asked her.

She nodded. She was prepared to support him in this decision. She knew he wouldn't be suggesting this option if he thought the baby would survive any other way. They may even be able to save both patients.

They pulled a fresh pair of surgical gloves on over the first.

Chloe tore open sterile packages containing surgical instruments and laid them on the seat beside her. She poured disinfectant liberally over the woman's abdomen, spreading it across her skin.

Xander picked up a scalpel and made a deep incision, slicing through the woman's abdomen from her umbilicus to her pubic bone. Blood was pooled in her abdominal cavity obstructing their vision. Chloe packed gauze into the abdomen, soaking up the blood, as Xander tied off an artery.

The blood was dealt with quickly and no more appeared. The woman remained unresponsive. Without a pulse she wasn't able to bleed.

Xander had his hands inside the woman's abdomen. He palpated her uterus, looking and feeling for signs of trauma.

Chloe knew he was making the right decision. If they didn't deliver this baby they would have two fatalities.

'The uterus is intact,' he said but it didn't remain that way for long.

Xander cut the uterus open and swiftly lifted the baby from the womb.

A boy.

He handed him to Chloe.

The whole procedure had taken less than four minutes.

'No meconium, cord intact and free, placenta intact,' Xander recounted while Chloe focused on her patient.

The baby was pink but flaccid. He wasn't crying. Or breathing. He had no reflexes on stimulus and his heart rate was well below ideal at just sixty beats per minute. He had a one-minute Apgar score of three out of ten. He was not out of danger yet.

Chloe dried the baby, rubbing him vigorously to warm him up and hopefully stimulate respiration. When that didn't work she wrapped him to keep him warm and prepared to suction his airway.

Xander was stitching the woman's abdomen but she saw him glance over at her.

'Do you need help?'

She nodded. 'He's not breathing. Pulse only sixty. Can you get ready to bag him?'

Xander ripped off his gloves before pulling on another clean pair. He grabbed a mask and attached the bag, placing the tiny mask over the baby's face when Chloe removed the suction tube.

The baby's heart rate remained low, despite the oxygen that was now being pumped into him.

'Swap places with me,' Xander instructed.

'What are you going to do?'

'Administer epinephrine.'

Xander didn't bother looking for a vein on the tiny struggling baby. He used an intraosseous needle, injecting the drug directly into the bone marrow in the tibia in an attempt to stimulate his heart.

Chloe kept bagging the newborn, holding her own breath as she waited for signs of improvement.

The five-minute Apgar score was three points better. The heart rate was above one hundred and the skin was pink-coloured. The reflexes were still absent and there was no grimace but there was spontaneous, albeit irregular, respiratory drive.

Chloe relaxed slightly but monitored the baby closely as Simon flew them to the hospital.

It was a flurry of activity from the moment they touched down on the helipad. The neonatal team whisked the baby away to the neonatal intensive care unit and Chloe followed. He wasn't her patient any longer but she needed to know he was going to be okay.

She waited while the neonatal team assessed the baby. It seemed wrong to leave him alone with no one to watch over him. His mother hadn't made it—she'd been declared deceased on arrival—and Chloe's heart went out to the tiny newborn who'd had such a traumatic introduction to the world.

Who was going to be responsible for this baby?

Her mind returned to the older woman she'd seen sitting in the back of the ambulance at the scene of the accident. She wondered where she was. Who she was. The grandmother? Had anyone told her what had happened to her family?

Chloe's mind drifted to her own daughter. Who would be there for Lily if something happened to her? Her mother? Her brothers?

Her mother was a young grandmother but raising another child on her own at her age? Chloe knew she'd do it but it wasn't right. And her brothers had their own lives to live.

Lily had a father. Chloe had Xander listed in her will. If anything should happen to her, she'd asked that he be found. But four years ago he hadn't wanted a family. Had things changed? Would he want Lily now?

Her thoughts were maudlin. Triggered by the day's events.

One life taken, one life saved. Chloe didn't know whether it had been a good day or a bad day.

It could have been better.

It could have been worse.

By the time the baby had been checked and given a relatively good prognosis her shift had ended and she could go home. She was surprised to find she was still wearing her flight overalls. They were covered in blood—she must look a complete mess. She couldn't leave the hospital like that.

She went upstairs to the air ambulance unit to change. Her hands were shaking as she stripped off the jumpsuit and tossed it into the laundry hamper. She stood still, gathering her thoughts, searching for the energy to turn around and go home.

She made it outside but couldn't make it much further than a bench overlooking the river. Her vision was blurry and her legs were weak.

She sat, letting the London commuters flow around her as they made their way home. She needed to give her wobbly knees a chance to rest and her brain a chance to reset. Her thoughts were disturbed, her mind circling. She couldn't seem to separate the baby's fate from her own past.

'Chloe, are you okay?'

She turned at the sound of his voice. Xander was standing beside the bench, his grey eyes shadowed, his brow furrowed with concern.

'Not really.' Her voice wobbled and her eyes filled with tears.

'Is it the baby?'

She shook her head. 'No, he's okay, but the mother didn't make it.'

'I heard.'

Chloe wiped her cheeks with the back of her hand. Her face was wet with tears. 'I'm sorry. I don't know why I'm upset.' But she did know. She was finding it hard to separate her life from their patients' today. She wasn't usually so affected by her work. By the tragedies. Normally she could compartmentalise.

Perhaps it had something to do with Xander's reappearance. She'd found herself unsettled, off-kilter, for the past few days. Her personal and professional lives were colliding. And today's events reminded her that she'd grown up without a parent and she'd put her daughter, Lily, in the same position.

'Don't apologise,' Xander said as he sat down next to her. 'Some jobs just get to us more than others.' He wrapped his arm around her, completely unaware of the direction of her thoughts.

Chloe leaned into him. She fitted perfectly into his side.

'You're freezing. Come on, you need to get out of the cold.'

Despite Xander's body heat she wasn't warming up. There was a breeze coming off the river and the spring evening was getting chilly now that the sun was setting.

He pulled her to her feet but kept his arm wrapped around her.

'Where are we going?'

'To get you warmed up. My flat is about five hundred metres along the river.'

She didn't argue. Her brain was too cold to stage a protest.

He walked on the river side of her along the Albert Embankment, keeping her sheltered from the wind, and guided her into a large, modern building overlooking the Thames. He kept her tucked against his side as they went up in the lift, almost as if he was afraid she would vanish if he let her go. He had no idea she was incapable of making any decisions at the moment. She had her eyes closed as she rested her head against his chest and listened to the sound of his heartbeat. Its steady rhythm was soothing, helping to settle her anxious mind.

She matched her steps to his, the thick carpet muffling their footsteps, as they crossed the corridor to his apartment. He swiped his card and held the door for her. A small entry foyer led into an open-plan living, dining, kitchen area on the left with, she assumed, a bedroom and bathroom to the right.

Xander switched on the lights and steered her towards a small couch. It was the only seating option aside from the dining chairs. She heard Xander flick the heating on and fill the kettle but her gaze was drawn to the bank of floor-to-ceiling windows. The apartment was modern, generic, impersonal but the view over the river was spectacular. She curled up on the couch and let her gaze wander over the

London skyline. The Houses of Parliament, Big Ben and the London Eye were spread out before her as the city lights began to glow as dusk deepened.

Xander placed a mug of coffee on the table in front of her but poured a nip of brandy into it before he passed it to her. He placed a plate of sweet biscuits on the table and sat beside her.

The couch seemed even smaller once Xander was sharing it with her. His thigh brushed against hers as he sat down and Chloe was tempted to climb into his lap. She made conversation to fill the silence, which she felt was becoming a little awkward.

'Did you notice the older lady at the scene of the accident?' she asked as she wrapped her hands around the mug to stop the shaking. Her hands felt like blocks of ice and she wondered if she'd ever feel warm again. 'The one who was in the back of the ambulance? Do you know who she was?'

'She was the baby's grandmother.'

'I wonder if she knows what has happened.'

'Is that what's bothering you?'

'Not just that.' Chloe shook her head. 'I've been wondering who is going to look after the baby. Does he have a father somewhere? Family. What if his grandmother is all he has?'

'At least he'll have someone.'

'He should have a mother. Better yet, he should have two parents.'

'We did everything possible, Chloe.'

'I know that. I'm not blaming anyone. It's just not the way things are meant to be.'

'There's absolutely no point worrying about things you can't change. I learnt that lesson a long time ago.'

'And I learnt the hard way that it's better to have two parents.'

'You did?'

Chloe nodded. 'I grew up without my father. He died when I was seven.'

Xander wrapped one arm around her shoulders and pulled her against his side. He held her quietly and his touch was reassuring. 'Do you want to tell me what happened?'

'He was a policeman, killed while on duty.'

'Oh, Chloe, that must have been tough.'

'It was.' She'd been angry at her father. He'd had an affair and had left her mother and his children. Chloe hadn't been able to understand how he could leave them all, how he could abandon her, and she hadn't forgiven him. And then he'd been killed responding to an armed robbery and she'd never had the chance to forgive him. She couldn't bring herself to tell Xander the full story right now; she still felt guilty about her anger. She didn't mention that he'd already abandoned them, had already walked out on them all to move in with his girlfriend, when he was killed. She tried not to think about that. She tried to forget that he'd chosen to leave them. She didn't subscribe to her mother's theory that he had left her but not his children. Her father had made a choice and she'd been left behind. 'Mum has raised us on her own.'

She had never told him any of this and talking about it now reminded her of how little they knew of each other. She had based her memories on a man who she'd possibly created in her imagination.

She went to sip her coffee and realised she'd finished it. She stared into her empty cup.

She was warming up but now she was restless. She jiggled her feet, making her knees jump up and down. She didn't like talking about her past. She should go home but she was reluctant to leave just yet.

Xander reached over and took the mug from her hands, placing it on the coffee table. 'You're still cold.' There was a small throw rug draped over the end of the couch. He pulled it towards him and wrapped it around her shoulders. She leant into him as he draped the blanket over her. She couldn't help it. She was drawn to him. She'd always been drawn to him.

'It's the one thing I can't get used to,' he continued as he held her hands. 'The cold. And the sense of space.'

'That's two things.'

'So it is.' He smiled and her feeling of hopelessness lifted.

'How long have you been away for?' she asked.

'Four years. On and off. Before Wales I was in Canada and in South Africa before that. I've been home on a couple of occasions but I've been gone for over twelve months this time. I was thinking about heading home once I finished here but…'

'But?'

He was rubbing her hands between his, warming them up. He stopped rubbing when she asked the question but he didn't let go of her.

'Now I'm not sure.' He was looking at her intently, his grey eyes serious and considerate. 'I don't believe in coincidences but I do believe in fate.'

She believed in fate too but she knew it could bring both good and bad fortune. Fate had introduced her to Xander and then taken her away from him.

Fate had given her Lily when she'd needed someone to love.

'I'm wondering if there's a reason we've found ourselves here together again,' he said.

Chloe was convinced there was a reason that Xander was back in her life. She just wasn't sure if he was going to *like* the reason. She had no idea if he was going to want to be a father. She knew this was an opportunity to tell him about Lily but she couldn't bring herself to start that discussion. She was exhausted, emotionally worn out, and she didn't think she could do justice to this conversation tonight. Xander seemed happy to talk so she stayed silent. She knew she was being a coward but it was the easier option.

He lifted her legs and rested them in his lap. He picked up her hand and kissed her fingertips. 'I've missed you.'

She wanted to tell him she'd missed him too. That she'd thought of him every day. But her voice caught in her throat. She was too afraid.

Her eyes filled with tears.

Had they wasted four years? Could they still be together? Could they have lasted?

He misunderstood her tears but she didn't care as he gathered her into his arms and stroked her hair. 'It's okay. It's just been a bad day. Everything will look better in the morning.'

It's the sort of thing she would say to Lily. The sort of thing her mother would say to her. The sort of thing a father might say.

But he didn't want children.

She let him comfort her anyway.

'Would you like to stay for dinner?' he asked. 'I'll order something in.'

She shook her head. 'I can't.' She couldn't stay. She couldn't risk it. There was too much at stake now.

She hadn't told her mother she'd be late and both Susan and Lily would be expecting her home soon if she didn't call. She wanted to be home in time to put Lily to bed. Lily was her priority. As much as she wanted to stay, Lily came first.

She had a daughter to get home to. Their daughter.

She was going to have to figure out how to tell him he was a father. She couldn't let this attraction go any further without telling him first. And she wanted to take this further. She knew it would happen. It was inevitable. Just like four years ago. Was her memory distorted by rose-tinted glasses? Tainted by her feelings for him as Lily's father? She didn't know but she knew she couldn't resist him. She didn't *want* to resist him.

'Can I see you over the weekend, then?' Xander's question jolted her out of her thoughts.

'One of my girlfriends is getting married in a couple of weeks. I'm a bridesmaid and we've a full day of preparations planned for tomorrow.'

'How about on Sunday?'

'I have a family thing.' But she couldn't leave without knowing that she'd see him again. 'I'd love to make plans—can I call you later and we'll sort something out?'

He nodded and said, 'Pass me your phone. I'll put my number in it.'

He stored his number in her phone and walked her out to hail a cab.

'I'll sit by the phone,' he said as he kissed her goodbye, 'waiting for your call.'

'You have a mobile. You can keep it with you.'

He grinned as she climbed into the cab. 'I'll still be waiting.'

Xander watched the tail lights of the cab fade into the distance, taking Chloe away. The ball was in her court now. Would she call him? Their chemistry hadn't faded; the spark between them was still bright. She had to feel it too. Would he get another chance?

He wanted a chance to get to know her again but this time he knew it would be different. Four years ago he hadn't been prepared for a serious relationship. He'd been emotionally, mentally and physically battered and bruised. A bit of a mess. She had been a bright light…one he hadn't wanted to dim by subjecting her to his tales of woe. She had lifted him out of his funk.

She'd changed his life in the short time that he'd known her. She'd brightened up his life, but he hadn't expected her to take some of that hope and light with her when she'd left. He'd expected that they'd have a brief affair and they would both move on with their lives. He hadn't been looking for anything more than what they'd shared. A brief physical encounter. It hadn't been until she'd gone that he'd realised how much he missed her. But he still hadn't been in a position to offer her anything.

She had changed him. But not enough.

He wished he hadn't let her go but, even now, he knew that had been the right thing to do.

Four years ago he hadn't been capable of getting into something where there would be an expectation of a long life. A family. All the things that normal people dreamt of. He had been looking short term then. Five years ahead. Not fifty.

But what about now? His life was different now. *He* was different.

He knew he had changed. He was in a better place emotionally. Not as wrung out. He'd recuperated and he was able to look to the future again. He was five years post-chemotherapy, four years divorced. He'd made peace with what had happened to him.

But peace was not happiness and he wanted to be happy again. The last time he'd been happy had been with Chloe.

He'd travelled the world since then searching for something. Searching for something to replace what she'd given him.

Happiness and hope.

He didn't have either of those things any more but was he expecting too much to hope that Chloe could or would give them back to him?

'How did your date go?'

Chloe pushed open the door to the bridal salon and was immediately accosted by Carly. For a moment she thought Carly was asking about Xander. She could still feel the imprint of Xander's hands on her skin, his lips on hers, and she could feel herself blushing before realising Carly was talking about Stephen. 'Are you bringing him to Esther's wedding?'

Chloe glanced at Esther. She had texted her to tell her that the date was a disaster. She mustn't have shared that information with Carly.

'I've given Esther the sack as a matchmaker.'

'Oh. What was the problem?'

She was blaming Esther, although she knew it wasn't her friend's fault. Stephen had been pleasant enough but he hadn't set her world on fire. In short, he hadn't made her feel like Xander did. 'We weren't compatible and I didn't want to waste his time, or mine.'

'You don't think you were being hasty?' Carly asked.

'No.' She shook her head. 'But it wasn't all bad,' she said as the shop assistant brought out armfuls of bridesmaid's dresses and arranged them on a rack.

The girls moved into one large change room and continued their conversation while they tried on the dresses, attempting to find something in a colour that suited them both and a style that flattered their figures.

'I actually ended up having a good night,' Chloe said as she stripped off her jeans and T-shirt.

'What? You went home alone. Has that become your definition of a good night?'

'I didn't go straight home.' She could see Carly's raised eyebrows as Esther zipped her into a pink dress. This was news to her.

'You didn't tell me that!'

'I figured you deserved to be fed information in small doses after the date you subjected me to,' Chloe told her. 'But then a guy at the bar offered to buy me a drink and I said yes.'

Chloe stepped into a bias cut, emerald green silk dress. Esther zipped up the dress. 'That colour isn't bad and the cut is flattering,' she said as Carly asked, 'Did you get his number? Will you see him again?'

Chloe nodded. 'Yes. He's just started work with the air ambulance. He's a doctor.' She didn't mention that he was from Australia. That she knew him before. That he was Lily's father. She wasn't ready for that conversation.

'I don't think I like the pink,' Esther said as she flicked through the racks and discarded anything floral or lace. 'I don't want anything that bright.' She turned back to Chloe. 'So, apart from work, will you see him again?'

'Yes.'

'When?'

'I'm not sure. I've got his number. I have to work out a time.'

'I'm organising drinks for Harry's birth-day this Thursday,' Esther said. 'Why don't you invite him to that? I'll make sure *not* to invite Stephen.'

Chloe had planned on having a date, just the two of them, but perhaps a social event was a good idea. She could get to know him again a little better first, have a casual con-versation, and she wouldn't feel pressured to mention Lily.

'I'll think about it,' she said before she turned her attention back to the task at hand. 'Now, what are we going to wear?'

'How about this?' Carly pulled a navy dress off the rack and held it up.

Esther smiled. 'Yes, that's perfect. I love it. Try it on.'

CHAPTER FIVE

'HAVING FUN?' ASKED Chloe's brother as he came to stand beside her.

Chloe was aware of some sideways glances from the other mums who had brought their children to the fire station open day as Guy stopped to talk to her. There was something about a man in uniform and Guy was tall, dark and handsome but Chloe knew he was also oblivious to the attention, totally besotted with his girlfriend of eighteen months.

'Lily is having an absolute blast,' she replied as she looked over to where Lily, wearing wellies, was stomping around in the puddles of water that had been left on the ground after the fire hose demonstration.

'I'm glad,' Guy told her, 'but I asked if *you* were having fun. This invitation was for you as well. I thought it would be a good way to introduce you to some of my single friends without it feeling like a set-up.'

Chloe was horrified. 'Why would you do that?'

'I've been wondering what your plans are. You're in danger of becoming an old lady before your time, staying home with Mum. You can't live with her for ever. You need some company your own age.'

'Don't you start!'

'What do you mean?'

'Everyone I know seems to be pushing me to date just because they've all found "the one." Carly and Adem, Esther and Harry, you and Hannah. You know I love the idea of being in love but I'm not like the rest of you. I'm not sure that I believe it can last for ever. It's hard to trust enough to give my heart away.' Especially when she'd done it once and it hadn't ended as she would have liked.

She hadn't planned to fall in love and it scared her how quickly she'd fallen for Xander. Her family thought she mistrusted men and was scared to love because of what happened with her father, but it was more than that. She'd been fearful to trust before meeting Xander and then when she met him all her defences were lowered. She'd fallen hard and fast. She had thought it was just a fling, an infatuation, and only later did she realise how serious she had been and how that fling tainted all other attempted relationships afterwards. Her reticence had less to do with her father and everything to do with Xander.

'Well, even if you don't want to date, what if Mum does? What if you're cramping her style?'

Chloe was aghast. She'd never even considered that she might be hindering her mother's social life. 'Has she said something to you?'

'No.' Guy laughed. 'I'm just stirring you up. But seriously, you can't stay tucked away with your mother and your daughter for the rest of your life.'

'I'm a bit preoccupied at the moment.'

'With what?'

She hesitated fractionally before deciding she could use his advice. Despite being four years younger than her Guy had an old head on his shoulders and he'd always had an emotional intelligence that she had sometimes envied. 'Xander is in London,' she told him. 'Working with the air ambulance team.'

'Xander? Australian Xander? As in...' Guy looked over to one of the fire engines where Lily was now sitting in the front seat beside her granny with a huge smile on her face.

'Yep.'

'Does he know?'

'Not yet.'

'You *are* going to tell him?'

'Of course I am. I'm just working out when.'

'What's the hold-up?'

'I don't want to spring it on him. It feels very sudden and abrupt to tell him when he's just arrived here.'

'What if Lily was the result of a one-night stand? Would you feel the same then? That you'd need to get to know the father better in that situation before you told him what had happened?'

'That's different.'

'Why?'

'Well, for one, I've never had a one-night stand so I can't imagine myself in that situation.' Even though she knew, the moment she met Xander, that she would sleep with him she waited until she knew it would be more than one night. She needed to get to know him first. She needed reassurance that he wasn't just going to sleep with her and run. 'And two, I'm not sure that I would tell them anything.'

'Really?'

'Would you want to know?' she asked.

'Of course. I have a responsibility. But I guess if Xander is in London, you've got some time to think about it but he has a right to know. If I were you I wouldn't wait too long.

He'll wonder why you haven't told him and I can't say I'd blame him.'

'I don't have all that long actually. He's only here for six weeks.'

And three of those weeks had already passed.

'You'd better spend some time with him, then. And quickly. If you like, why don't the four of us have dinner together?'

'Me, Xander, you and Hannah?' She assumed Guy was including his girlfriend in the group of four. 'Why?'

'I'd like to meet him and that gives you a reason to invite him out. Although Hannah is flat out with her final placement and studying for her final exams. Maybe we should ask Tom instead.'

'No!' Chloe panicked at the thought of *both* her brothers quizzing Xander. 'He'd feel like he was at the Spanish Inquisition. Hannah has to eat—maybe we could have a quick dinner one night. How is she feeling about her exams?'

'I'm actually a bit worried about her. She seems unusually uptight. She's very tired and not sleeping well. She seems a bit under the weather generally but I'm not sure what I can do to help.'

'Has she been to the doctor? It could be a virus, glandular fever.'

'She says it's just stress.'

'Is she eating properly?'

'I think so. Her mum does most of the cooking so I know she at least has one proper meal a day because it's made for her.'

'Maybe we *should* organise dinner,' she said as she saw her mum returning with Lily. 'I can have a chat to her then if you like and see if I can't persuade her to see a doctor.'

'That would be good. I'm looking forward to the next few months being over. Hopefully things will go back to normal.'

Xander was pleased to get to work. He wanted to be busy. It stopped him thinking about Chloe. About how many hours had passed since he'd seen her. About how she'd said she would call but he still hadn't heard from her. He had her number but he didn't want to pressure her, although he was running out of time. He was already halfway through his stint in London. Granted, he could extend his stay— he had a working visa—but he knew the only reason he would stay was for Chloe.

His plan had been to go home once he finished up in London; he'd been away from home long enough. He hadn't found what he was looking for until now. And if Chloe didn't want to pursue things further with him there was no reason for him to stay.

He strapped himself into the chopper and concentrated on the job, listening as Jeff relayed the scant information they had received.

'Unconscious twenty-two-year-old female. Mother found her seizing on the bathroom floor. No history of epilepsy.'

Xander looked down at the city. He loved the view from the air. Loved taking a moment to relax. He took a deep breath as he mentally prepared for whatever came next. That was the thing with this job—he never really knew what he was about to encounter. The flight to the emergency always offered a moment of peace and calm.

The River Thames shone silver in the pale morning sun, lines of white disturbing the surface as the wakes of the boats disrupted the water. The commuting traffic was at a standstill below them as they banked right and he knew the commuters were probably feeling anything but calm and peaceful. Flying over the city was so different to the flights he'd taken with the flying doctor back home. The grey and green and silver of London contrasted sharply with the ochre, brown and turquoise of the Australian outback.

The chopper started circling and Xander switched back into the present, knowing they were about to land.

'She's in here.'

Their patient was lying on the bathroom floor. She was unconscious but someone—Xander assumed her mother—had put her into the coma position. She had been bleeding from a cut on her head and the blood had dried on her cheek and stuck in her dark hair.

She was dressed in track pants and a loose T-shirt. She looked cold but when Xander placed his hand on her bare arm he could feel heat radiating from her even through his gloves. Her face was flushed. Feverish.

He could see her chest rising and falling so, although unconscious, she was at least still breathing.

He turned to the woman's mother as Rick knelt beside the patient and started checking her vital signs.

'Can you tell me what happened?' he asked as Rick wrapped a cuff around the woman's arm to check her blood pressure.

The mother stood in the doorway of the bathroom, wringing her hands. 'When she went to bed last night she said she wasn't feeling well. I checked her later and she was sleeping and then this morning I heard her fall. When I came into the bathroom she was having a seizure. I haven't been able to wake her.'

Her eyes filled with tears and she looked worried. Xander could understand her concern; he was worried too, but he tried not to show it.

Xander squatted down and lifted one of the woman's eyelids. He shone a torch into her eye and her pupil contracted. He repeated the process on the other eye with the same result. He breathed out and relaxed slightly. She didn't appear to have sustained a head injury.

'She's never had a seizure before?' he asked. 'No family history of epilepsy?'

The mother shook her head.

'BP one-five-four over ninety-nine,' Rick reported as he clipped an oximeter onto the patient's finger before taking her temperature.

Damn. Her blood pressure was dangerously high.

'Not feeling well, how?' Xander asked the woman's mother. 'Nausea? Vomiting? Headaches?'

'A headache and a stomach ache. I'm not sure if she was nauseous but she hasn't vomited.'

'Heart rate ninety-two BPM; oxygen sats

ninety-seven per cent.' Rick passed on more information.

'Had she been drinking?' Xander queried.

The mother shook her head. 'No. She's been studying for final exams. I thought it was stress but then I heard her get up before I heard a crash. When I went into the bathroom it looked like she was fitting.'

Xander continued his assessment as he listened to the mother. There was oedema in the woman's hands and feet, the swelling very obvious, given how thin her limbs were. He slid a stethoscope under her T-shirt and listened to her chest. Her breathing was irregular, her heartbeat rapid.

Rick was holding leads in his hand. He was looking at Xander, ready to attach them to their patient. Xander nodded and Rick proceeded to stick the ECG leads on.

Despite the woman's slim build her abdomen was distended.

Xander palpated her abdomen as he waited for the ECG to record the heart rhythm. It was round and tight with noticeable firmness in the right upper quadrant over the liver. The patient's temperature was elevated; she had no history of seizures and hadn't been drinking. He paused, considering the signs.

'Could she be pregnant?' he asked.

'Pregnant? No.'

'Are you sure?' The patient was the right age and the signs all fitted. She could be suffering from pre-eclampsia, but *only* if she was pregnant.

'Yes. She's been having her period as far as I know.'

'ECG is normal,' Rick said.

Had Xander made the signs fit his diagnosis? He didn't think so. It made sense.

He still had one hand resting on the woman's abdomen. He felt something move under his palm and he was almost certain it was a foot or elbow. Which would mean that, despite the mother's conviction, their patient *was* pregnant.

He slipped the stethoscope back into his ears and held it to the woman's abdomen, listening this time for a foetal heartbeat.

He found a heartbeat and counted the beats.

One hundred and thirty-five BPM.

He double-checked the woman's heart rate. It was still ninety-two.

He was sure he was right.

'Can you set up IV glucose?' he asked Rick. 'And I'll also administer precautionary antibiotics. We need to take bloods for liver function and kidney function testing and then I want her in the chopper. She needs an ultrasound and we need to get her to the hospital.'

'What's going on?' the patient's mother asked.

Xander tightened the tourniquet around the woman's arm, ready to draw blood, as he spoke to the mother. 'I think there's a high possibility that your daughter is pregnant.' He realised he may be breaking confidentiality but, if he was correct, her condition was life-threatening. 'It's probable that she has a condition called pre-eclampsia. If I'm right the only way to resolve it is to deliver the baby. Which means performing an emergency Caesarean. We need to get her to hospital and I need to know, do I have your permission to provide whatever treatment we deem necessary to save her life?' He saw the colour drain from the mother's face as she digested his words. She nodded, numbly, as he said, 'I realise this is a shock and this is all extremely overwhelming but time is of the essence.'

Chloe stood on the helipad, surrounded by colleagues from the A&E. She heard the thump of the chopper blades and shaded her eyes, watching it approach above the city skyline.

The fire crew slid the door open as it touched down and Chloe's heart rate accelerated when Xander jumped out. Even though she'd been expecting to see him she couldn't control her reaction. Every time the sight of him made her buzz with anticipation.

Rick followed Xander out of the chopper and Chloe moved forward with everyone else who had been waiting, and met Xander and Rick halfway.

Xander handed a cooler bag to one of the nurses. 'I need kidney and liver function tests, please—stat,' he said before relaying the information he had to the rest of the medical team. Chloe had heard some of it before but the information was limited at best.

'We have a twenty-two-year-old female. She had a seizure and is now unconscious. BP one-fifty over ninety, but it was higher. Febrile. We've administered IV antibiotics.'

An oxygen mask covered the patient's face and an IV line snaked into her left arm.

'She's pregnant,' Xander continued, 'and I'm betting on the problem being pre-eclampsia. I think she's close to term.'

'You *think*?'

Xander nodded. 'Her mother had no knowledge of a pregnancy. We have no antenatal history and an unconscious patient. I did a fundal measurement and the baby seems a healthy size and certainly past thirty-four weeks.'

Chloe was standing at the patient's feet. From that angle she could see a slightly rounded abdomen, very slight. She certainly didn't look full term but she looked tall and she was young. Chloe knew strong abdominal muscles could keep a pregnancy disguised for some time, especially a first pregnancy. If Xander was right the baby's lung development wouldn't be a concern. But what if he was wrong?

'She needs an ultrasound scan. We didn't have time on board, and we need those blood test results. If she's pregnant you'll need to deliver the baby.'

'Raphael Dubois is waiting. He's one of our obstetricians,' Chloe told Xander as they pushed the stretcher into the hospital and into the lift that would take them straight to the theatres. 'Have we got consent to operate?' she asked as the lift doors closed.

'Yes. From the mother.'

The doors slid open and Chloe stepped out, pulling the foot of the stretcher with her. Theatre staff crowded around them and the patient was quickly transferred.

The team rapidly disconnected and reconnected monitors and equipment. As the oxygen masks were swapped over Chloe did a double take.

'Oh, my God. Hannah!'

'You know her?' Raphael asked.

Chloe nodded.

'Are you all right to be the attending midwife?'

'Yes, I'll be fine,' she said. She'd be okay. She could do this. There was no reason why she couldn't be the attending midwife. She just needed to focus.

Anyway, surely Hannah wasn't really pregnant? Surely she and Guy would have shared that news with the family. Xander must have made a mistake.

Unless Guy didn't know?

Maybe it wasn't his?

No. She blocked that thought out. If Hannah was pregnant there had to be a logical explanation.

She had no more time to think. She had a job to do.

But although Xander had vanished in the ensuing chaos he hadn't made a mistake. Hannah was pregnant and close to full term.

'Liver enzymes are elevated and platelet count is low.' Hannah's blood work was back and apparently Xander hadn't made *any* mistakes. His diagnosis was spot on. Hannah was suffering from pre-eclampsia and the only way to resolve this condition was to deliver the baby.

Hannah was prepped for surgery and sedated for Raphael to perform a Caesarean section. Within minutes he had delivered a healthy baby boy.

The baby was passed to Chloe to be cleaned and weighed and checked before the paediatrician gave him a more thorough examination.

His one-minute Apgar score was an eight and he weighed six pounds and ten ounces. He certainly looked close to full term, Chloe thought as she wiped him over with warm water.

She searched his face as she gently wiped around his eyes and nose, looking for any trace of her brother in the baby's features. She knew she was being silly. All babies looked the same. It was an old midwives' tale that they all looked like their fathers in order to persuade the fathers to bond with them. But was this baby her nephew?

If so, why hadn't Guy said anything?

The question nagged at her, refusing to go away as she waited for the paediatrician to finish her checks.

She took the baby back, swaddled him and placed him in a crib to be taken to the neonatal ICU for monitoring. The moment she handed over his care to the neonatal team she headed for her locker and pulled out her phone. She left a message for her brother. Regardless of her concerns someone needed to let Guy know where Hannah was.

Chloe had been pacing the floors in A&E since the end of her shift, waiting for Guy. He eventually burst through the automatic doors, still in his fireman's uniform, his brow furrowed with concern. She saw him scan the waiting area, looking for her, and she walked towards him.

She wrapped her arms around him in a tight hug as he said, 'What's happened? Is Hannah all right?'

Chloe's message had just told him that Hannah had been brought into hospital but that she would be okay, and she asked him to meet her here as soon as possible. She hadn't mentioned the baby. That information wasn't something she was comfortable putting into a message.

'She will be.'

'Where is she?' His eyes continued to scan the waiting area as if he thought his girlfriend might be sitting in a chair.

Chloe steered him into a side room, one of the rooms they used when they needed to have a private conversation in A&E. Often those conversations did not go well and she could see Guy looking around nervously. She sat him down. 'She's in ICU. She needed surgery.'

'Surgery? What happened?' he repeated.

There was no easy way to approach this. Chloe had been racking her brain all afternoon trying to work out how to start this conversation but hadn't come up with anything subtle or gentle. 'Did you know she was pregnant?'

'What? Pregnant? No? Is that why she's been feeling unwell?' He paused and then added in a quieter voice, 'Has she had a miscarriage?'

'No. She's had a baby.'

'What? A baby?' Guy stared at her. 'Are you sure?'

'I'm positive. I was there at the delivery.' She paused but continued when Guy didn't ask any further questions. She assumed shock was setting in. 'Hannah collapsed at home. She had a seizure and was unconscious. She was brought in with the air ambulance. Xander suspected that she was pregnant and suffering from pre-eclampsia. The baby was delivered via C-section.'

'A baby.' He sounded incredulous. Not that Chloe could blame him. 'Is it okay?'

'He's perfect.'

'It's a boy?'

'Yes.'

'And Hannah is okay too?'

Chloe nodded.

She saw Guy's shoulders relax and he smiled before asking, 'Can I see them?'

His request surprised her and she wondered why he hadn't asked any more questions. Perhaps the shock was numbing his brain. He certainly wasn't questioning the baby's parentage.

Her mind wandered and her silence obviously had Guy worried. He looked as though he was expecting her to say no.

She nodded again as she handed him a pair of clean scrubs. 'You can but you need to wash your hands and face first and put these on. You can't go into the nursery or into ICU covered in dirt. You can leave your uniform in a locker and pick it up later.'

She waited for him to change and then took him to the nursery. The baby was healthy and hadn't needed to go into the neonatal unit but, even so, she couldn't let Guy go alone—she needed to vouch for him. She needed to tell the nurses on duty that Guy was the baby's father, even if she wasn't certain of that herself.

The nurse congratulated Guy and led them to a row of cribs.

'This one?' Guy asked as he gazed down at

the baby. He seemed happy if somewhat quiet and stunned.

Chloe nodded.

'He doesn't look like a premmie.'

'He's not,' Chloe replied. 'We think Hannah must have been at least thirty-seven weeks.'

Guy was staring at her. *'Thirty-seven weeks? How is that possible?* I didn't even know she was pregnant.'

'Apparently Hannah's mother didn't know either. And when I last saw Hannah—what, a month ago?—I didn't notice anything and she must have been at least seven months pregnant then.'

'Why would she keep it a secret?'

There was only one reason Chloe could think of and her silence obviously led Guy to the same conclusion but he wasn't having a bar of it. 'Don't say it. He's definitely mine. Hannah wouldn't cheat on me.'

Chloe held her tongue. It wasn't any of her business. If Guy trusted Hannah, if he believed the baby was his—and at this stage Chloe had no reason to think he wasn't—then that was all that mattered. Which meant there was one other possible explanation.

'Maybe she didn't know either,' Chloe said.

'How could *she* not know she was pregnant?'

'It does happen.' She thought that was unlikely but not impossible. 'She's tall, fit, with good abdominal tone. The baby had room to hide in her abdominal cavity. And,' she continued, 'some women continue to experience light bleeding throughout pregnancy, which is a bit of a red herring. Obviously it's unexpected, so even though Hannah hadn't been feeling well lately she might not have considered pregnancy as the reason behind it.'

'You think *that's* why she's been under the weather? Not stress.'

'I don't know but it's possible.' Unusual but still possible, Chloe thought as she let herself relax. She might have jumped to all the wrong conclusions. The easiest explanation wasn't always the right one.

'Do you want to hold him?' she asked.

'Can I?'

'Of course.' Chloe picked up the baby and handed him to Guy.

'He's beautiful.'

Chloe had to agree. He was a gorgeous baby. Not red or wrinkled, not overcooked or underweight. Chloe was sure he was close to full term but his head must not have engaged in Hannah's pelvis as it was perfectly shaped and had stayed that way because he was delivered via Caesarean section.

Chloe remembered how it felt to hold your own child for the first time. The weight of your own flesh and blood in your arms, the amazing, overwhelming sense of love and awe. The realisation that you would do anything you had to to protect them from harm.

Guy had that same look of wonder on his face. He looked so young but at twenty-three he was about the same age as Chloe had been when she'd unexpectedly found herself a parent and she had managed. And she knew Guy would be a good father.

'Can I see Hannah now?'

Chloe nodded. 'You go up to ICU. I'll take care of this little one,' she said as she held her arms out to take the baby. 'Hannah's mum should be there. She will have to wait outside and give you permission to see her. It's only one family member at a time.'

'You're not coming?'

Chloe shook her head. 'I need to go home. Mum's got Lily. Will you come past later? Stay for dinner? I think you should have company tonight.'

'Okay. Thanks. For everything.'

Guy hugged her and headed for the stairwell. Chloe cuddled the baby for a while longer before returning him to his crib and heading for the lift. It had been a long and taxing day and she was looking forward to getting home.

The lift doors opened, revealing one occupant.

Xander.

The sight of him brought her close to tears. She'd had a stressful day and her emotions were running high.

'Are you okay?'

'Not really. It's been a crazy day.'

Her voice wobbled with exhaustion and she really needed a hug. She was tempted to step into his arms but instead she leaned back on the wall of the lift, out of reach of temptation.

'What's going on?' he asked.

'It turned out that the woman you brought in earlier is my brother's girlfriend.'

'The pregnant one?'

Chloe nodded.

'Did you know she was pregnant?' Xander asked.

'No. And neither did Guy.'

'So is it his baby?'

'He says it must be.'

'Do you believe him?'

She knew what he was thinking even though his thoughts remained unspoken. She squashed her sense of slight irritation; she couldn't get cross with him as she'd had the same thought. 'It's not my place not to,' she said.

'How is the baby?'

'He's fine. Perfect.'

'It was a boy?'

'Yes.'

'And the mother? Your brother's girlfriend?'

'She's in ICU but she's stable. You saved two lives today.' She smiled. 'Thank you.'

'It's what we do,' he replied. 'How is Guy coping?'

Chloe shrugged. 'He's in shock. Stunned. We all are.'

'It's not every day you discover you're an instant father.'

'No.' Chloe was quiet, wondering if she should tell him her news now.

No.

Now was not the time. She didn't have the energy for that discussion. That wouldn't be fair on either of them. Now was not the time *or* the place. She was beginning to wonder if there really wasn't ever going to be the perfect time. Maybe she'd just have to bite the bullet and have the conversation. Get it over and done with.

'Will he do a DNA test?' Xander asked.

'I have no idea. I don't think that's even crossed his mind. Is that what you would do?'

Chloe's heart was beating rapidly and she was having difficulty breathing as she waited for his answer.

'Maybe. Probably.'

His answer wasn't unreasonable but it wasn't the answer she wanted to hear.

A shadow passed behind his grey eyes and she wondered if he'd been in the same position. Was that why his marriage broke up? She couldn't help but feel sympathy for him based on nothing but his expression and the sadness in his eyes. That troubled look in his eyes was so familiar. She hadn't noticed it as much over the last week but it was back again now, that slightly haunted look that never failed to draw her in.

The lift doors opened at the ground floor. She couldn't believe no one else had got in.

'Would you like to go for that drink now?' he asked as they stepped out.

'I can't.'

'I know I said I'd leave it up to you but we're running out of time and you look like you could really use a drink.'

'I have to go home. Mum and my other brother are waiting. I need to let them know what's been happening. But if you're free on Thursday I'm going out with some friends from here—just a small group, my best friends, really—and they've asked me to bring you.' She knew she should stay away but she couldn't.

'Really?'

She nodded. It was safer than having drinks with him alone. It gave her an excuse to see him without giving her the opportunity to divulge her secret. She knew she couldn't avoid that discussion for ever but maybe this could buy her a few more days. She was terrified of what might happen next.

'Shall I pick you up?' he offered.

'No!' There was no way she was having him turn up at her house. 'We're going to a pub for birthday drinks. The pub is closer to you. I'll meet you at your place.'

'Chloe?' Shirley stuck her head into a treatment cubicle where Chloe was giving her patient her discharge instructions. 'Do you think you could take your break when you're finished here? Hannah is asking to see you.'

'She's conscious?'

Shirley nodded. 'She's been moved to the maternity ward.'

Everyone in the hospital had heard Hannah's story, patient confidentiality didn't seem to extend to surprise births.

As Chloe made her way upstairs she wondered if Guy knew Hannah had woken up. He'd been into the hospital first thing today to see the baby and Hannah but she'd still been in high dependency then.

She could see Hannah's mother pacing the corridor outside her daughter's room. She held a baby in her arms.

'Chloe. Thank you for coming,' Pam said.

'Hey, little man,' Chloe said as she reached out and stroked her nephew's cheek. He was sleeping, blissfully unaware of all the drama surrounding his birth. She lifted her head and looked at Hannah's mum. 'How is Hannah doing, Pam?'

'Physically okay, the doctors tell me, but she's very agitated. The nurses brought the baby in to her and she got very distressed. She's insisting he isn't hers.'

'What?' Chloe had thought of a dozen different explanations for this surprise baby but she hadn't expected Hannah to deny the baby was hers.

'I don't know what to do.' Pam's face was lined with worry. 'She seems very confused but the doctors have said she's recovering well. I wondered if you might be able to have a chat with her. I thought seeing as she knows you, and Guy told me you were there for the delivery, Hannah might listen to you.'

'Okay, I'll see how I go.' She stroked the baby's cheek one more time, then went into Hannah's room.

'Chloe! Thank God,' Hannah greeted her.

She looked pale but otherwise okay. She was still connected to various monitors and an IV line ran into her arm but she was obviously coherent enough to recognise Chloe.

'Can you tell me what's happening, Chloe?'

'Of course. What do you remember?'

'I remember going to bed and then I woke up here, in hospital. I've got stitches in my stomach but no one will tell me what happened. Was I in an accident?'

What did she mean no one would tell her what happened? Was Hannah confused? Did she have short-term memory loss? Did she even remember being told she'd had a baby?

'You collapsed at home yesterday.'

Hannah frowned. 'Yesterday? What day is it?'

'Monday,' said Chloe gently. 'You'd been complaining of headaches but you had a seizure and your blood pressure was dangerously high. You were brought into hospital by the ambulance. You had pre-eclampsia.'

'Pre-what?'

'It's a condition associated with pregnancy. We had to deliver your baby.'

Hannah shook her head. 'Why does everyone keep talking about a baby? I don't have a baby!'

'Hannah.' Chloe sat in the chair beside the bed. 'I was there when you were brought into the hospital. I was there in the operating room. I was there when you had a Caesarean section.'

'A Caesarean section?'

'Yes. That's why you have stitches in your stomach.'

'But I wasn't pregnant!'

Chloe took her hand. 'Hannah, I promise, you've had a baby. I was there when the surgeon delivered him.'

'No.' Hannah shook her head again and Chloe could tell she was close to tears. 'I must be dreaming. Surely I'd know if I was pregnant. I'm not stupid.'

Chloe knew it was possible that Hannah hadn't known. She needed to give her the benefit of the doubt. In her distressed state she didn't need any other pressure. She sat on the bed and gently wrapped her arms around Hannah. 'Shh. You need to relax. Your body and your mind need time to recover. It will take time to get your head around this but it will be okay. Everything will be all right.'

'How can you say that?' Hannah's shoulders shook as she cried. 'This doesn't make any sense.'

'I know,' Chloe reassured her. 'I know it sounds crazy but I promise I'm telling you the truth. You have a healthy baby boy.'

She felt Hannah take a deep breath and her sobs stilled. 'You're telling me the truth? I really have a son?'

'You do. You have a beautiful, healthy baby boy. Would you like to see him?'

Chloe stepped out of the room when Hannah nodded and spoke to Pam. She took the baby from his grandmother's arms and carried him in to Hannah. He was tiny but perfect and Chloe's heart swelled with love. There was something so precious about newborn babies and, when they were family too, it didn't get better than that. Chloe would love more children of her own but, for now, she'd enjoy her nephew.

'Do you want to hold him?' Chloe asked as she held him out to Hannah, but Hannah shook her head and kept her arms folded across her chest, refusing to take him.

'I don't know what to do with a baby.'

Chloe cuddled the baby back into her chest. She was convinced that once Hannah held him she'd sense he belonged to her and would be as besotted as everyone else was. But she couldn't force her to take him.

'I know this is scary,' Chloe said. She knew Hannah would still be in shock and Chloe couldn't imagine how she must be feeling. To have no idea she was pregnant and to wake up being told she was a mum would floor anyone. Hannah had also missed out on all the joy and wonder of a pregnancy. Expectant mums usually had months to get used to the idea, months to make plans, months for the excitement to build and months of anticipation of holding their baby for the first time. Hannah had none of that. She must be feeling overwhelmed. 'But you have our support. You and this little fellow are Guy's family now. Our family.'

'Does Guy know where I am?' Hannah asked.

Chloe nodded. 'He's been in to see you. He was here last night and again this morning.'

'He knows about the baby?' Hannah looked worried.

'Yes.'

'What did he say?'

Chloe realised that was what she was concerned about. She was worried that Guy wouldn't want the baby.

'He thinks his son is amazing. He thinks you're amazing,' Chloe reassured her. 'It'll be okay. Guy isn't going anywhere.'

'Are you sure?'

Chloe nodded. 'Do you want to hold him now? See how he feels. Smell him. There's nothing like the smell of a newborn baby.'

Hannah nodded this time and held out her arms, cradling him against her. 'He's really mine?'

'Yes.'

She stared down at the sleeping bundle.

'How could I not know that I was pregnant?'

'Some women have very straightforward, uncomplicated pregnancies. It's not an illness. But you would have had some changes to your body. Do you think you might have noticed some and attributed them to something else?' Chloe knew Hannah would be feeling foolish and she tried to give her a reasonable explanation.

'Like what?'

'Weight gain? Tiredness? Irritability?'

'I'd put on a little bit of weight but I haven't been exercising as much lately and I had a headache for the past week but I put that down to stress over my exams. Oh, my God!' Hannah looked up at Chloe. 'My exams! What will I do about those?'

Chloe thought that was probably the least of Hannah's concerns at the moment but she realised it was something she'd been working towards for months and it would seem like a big deal. 'I'll organise for a counsellor to come and speak to you. I'm sure there's a way of re-scheduling or postponing your exams,' Chloe said as she saw Guy arrive. She kissed Hannah goodbye and left the room, allowing Guy and Hannah some privacy. Hannah needed to spend time with him and their son. She needed to know that everything would be okay.

Guy had looked happy as he'd traded places with Chloe. He'd missed out on the excitement of the pregnancy too. Chloe knew from her own experience dealing with expectant fathers that many of them enjoyed the excitement and anticipation of a pregnancy as much as the mothers.

She wondered if Xander would have enjoyed the experience. Would he have changed his mind about having children if he was presented with a done deal? Would he have been excited? Would he have wanted to be involved? To experience it all or would he have remained distant? Surely he would have changed his mind? She hoped he would have. Surely he would have wanted to share the experience? Surely he would have wanted his daughter?

CHAPTER SIX

CHLOE PRESSED THE doorbell for Xander's apartment and checked her outfit in the mirror in the building's hallway. She fluffed her hair out over her shoulders as she waited for him to answer. She'd washed it and let it air dry, deliberately allowing it to curl wildly, knowing he loved her to wear it down.

She'd had the day off work but had spent it with Hannah, who had been discharged from hospital and was now home and trying to adjust in to her new role as a mother to baby Jonas. The week had been crazy and Chloe was looking forward to tonight. She was looking forward to talking and thinking about something else other than babies. She was looking forward to seeing Xander and pretending that she was four years younger, with no responsibilities and nothing better to do than go out for a drink with a handsome man.

His door swung open and he stood before her. He was still tugging his grey T-shirt down over his chest, obviously still getting ready, and she caught a glimpse of his belly button and taut abdominals. She swallowed; suddenly she was nervous. 'Am I early?'

'No.' His eyes travelled the length of her body and she was rewarded with a large smile. 'You're perfect.' She had dressed carefully, choosing white jeans and a gauzy, pink and white floral, off-the-shoulder top. She knew she was tempting fate but she was excited about tonight and wanted to make an impression.

He didn't invite her in. He stepped into the hall and cupped her face in his hands, bending his head to hers, and greeted her with a kiss.

Her body felt as if it was exploding into a thousand tiny pieces. He just had to look at her to set her heart racing and once his lips met hers she could barely stand. Her toes tingled and her legs felt like jelly. She was immediately transported back four years. To when they couldn't keep their hands off each other. To when she had nothing to worry about—other than not getting pregnant.

That hadn't worked out so well.

She pulled back as that thought made its way out of her subconscious. She couldn't afford to get carried away. She couldn't afford to get too involved. Things were not so simple any more.

'Have we got time for a drink here before we go?' Xander asked. If he noticed her withdrawal, he didn't mention it. She nodded and he held the door for her as they stepped inside.

'Gin and tonic?'

'Thanks.' Chloe leant on the kitchen bench as he mixed her drink. This felt normal, comfortable, and she was able to relax a little.

'How has your week been? How are Hannah and your new nephew doing?' he asked as he handed her a glass. She hadn't seen him for three days. There had been no emergencies that had involved her on Tuesday and she'd had the past two days rostered off. It felt far longer than three days though; it felt like a lifetime.

She took her drink and followed Xander to the small couch. 'It's been absolutely crazy. But Hannah is doing well all things considered. I can't imagine having no warning that you're going to have a baby.' Chloe had found it hard enough to cope with a surprise pregnancy; she couldn't imagine having to cope with a surprise baby.

'Lucky for them you've got some experience with babies.'

'Mmm-hmm, I guess it is.' She had more experience than he knew but she wasn't ready to talk about Lily yet.

'And Hannah really had no idea she was pregnant?'

'Apparently. She'd had headaches and a few warning signs for pre-eclampsia but she was studying for her final exams and she put it down to stress. She said she never skipped a period and didn't have any morning sickness.'

'And what about your brother? How is he coping?'

'They have a lot to sort out but luckily there doesn't seem to be any issue over paternity. Their situation is stressful enough without any of those questions. They trust each other and they've been in a relationship for a while, even though this is a bit more serious than they had planned at this stage.'

'How old is your brother?'

'Twenty-three.'

'Is he ready for this?'

'I don't know if anyone is ever really ready. I see so many first-time parents—most of them have no idea. Age is just a number and I know Guy would never, ever, walk away from his child.'

'How can you be so sure?'

'Guy was only three when our father died

and Tom was just a baby. The boys don't remember him and I know that has affected Guy. He would want his child to know him and even if he and Hannah weren't so solid I know he'd always make his child a priority.' She very nearly said, *He's so good with Lily*, but she stopped herself just before she could say something she couldn't take back.

'You have two brothers? Guy and...'

'Tom.' She nodded. 'What about you? Who's in your family?'

'Both my parents are still alive—they'll celebrate their fortieth wedding anniversary this year.'

Forty years! She wondered if they were happily married. If they'd had their share of ups and downs.

'And I have three older sisters,' Xander added. 'And four nieces and nephews.'

Lily had cousins on Xander's side as well. It was strange... Chloe hadn't imagined that. Lily had a whole other family. 'And one ex-wife.'

'Yes.'

'Would you get ever get married again?'

'I'd like to think so. I don't want to imagine spending the rest of my life alone. I always saw myself as a husband and father.'

'You want children?'

'Definitely.'

'Oh.' Chloe stood up and took her empty glass to Xander's compact kitchen as she digested that information. Somewhere along the line she'd got her wires crossed. He wanted kids. That changed everything.

'You seem surprised,' he said.

'I thought you said you and your wife split up because she wanted kids. I guess I assumed that meant you didn't.'

'It was a bit more complicated than that.' He glanced at his watch but not before Chloe saw the shadow pass across his eyes again. 'Should we go?' He stood up and grabbed his keys and it was clear that conversation was over.

Chloe nodded, happy to change tack. She needed a few moments to get her head straight.

'Just remind me who's going to be at the pub,' he said as he locked his front door behind them.

'It's Harry's birthday—he's marrying my friend Esther—and Carly, my other best friend, and her fiancé, Adem, will be there too. Harry and Adem are both doctors. I guess there will be a few doctors there so you'll have plenty to talk about besides weddings.'

'Your two best friends are both engaged? What about you? No serious relationships in the past four years?'

She shook her head. 'I've been too busy.'

'Doing what?'

'Doing everything I needed to get into the air ambulance service. I've been working at the Queen Victoria since I got back from Australia with the goal of becoming one of the midwives for the air ambulance. It took me a few years but I've been working with them now for the past twelve months. I love it but that has been my focus.'

That, and raising a child.

She was slightly relieved to see the pub ahead of them; intimate conversations were unlikely to be had once they were amongst her friends. She had almost mentioned Lily twice. She was such a big part of her life—she *was* her life—and outside of work Lily was her number one focus and, she realised, her number one topic of conversation. She'd have to be careful or she'd need to avoid Xander until she worked out what to say and how to tell him or, alternatively, she'd need to tell him about Lily pronto.

She didn't want to avoid him—she longed to spend more time with him—but that meant she would have to tell him her news. She couldn't, in good conscience, keep it from him any longer. She'd tell him tonight, she decided, after the drinks. She'd delayed the inevitable long enough and all this secrecy was becoming stressful. She'd go with him back to his flat after drinks and talk to him then.

She breathed out and relaxed, relieved to have made the decision.

'Is everything all right?' Xander asked as they reached the pub. 'You've gone very quiet.'

She looked up at him, into his grey eyes that were a reflection of Lily's. 'Yes.' She nodded. He wanted children. She had to believe that everything would be all right. She needed to stop worrying about things that were out of her control.

She stepped inside, followed by Xander. She could see her friends standing together near the fireplace at the far end of the bar. Harry, Esther, Raphael and Adem were chatting. Carly was on the phone. Chloe made the introductions while Carly finished her conversation.

Carly was buzzing with excitement when she ended her call and, while she let Chloe introduce her to Xander, Chloe could tell she had other things on her mind.

'Guess who's coming back in time for my wedding?' Carly said.

'Whose wedding?' Adem teased her.

'*Our* wedding,' Carly said as she tucked

her arm through the crook of his elbow and beamed at him, placating him.

'Who?'

'Izzy!'

'Really! That's brilliant,' Chloe said.

'I wish she could be here for ours,' Esther chimed in, 'but this is the next best thing.'

'You've just gone from triple trouble to quadruple trouble, my friend,' Harry said to Adem.

Chloe noticed that Raphael, who was also a close friend of Izzy's, was the only one in the group who didn't seem surprised. 'Izzy is the fourth musketeer,' Chloe explained to Xander. 'Carly, Esther, Izzy and I all studied midwifery together but Izzy has been gone for a while. She's a Kiwi originally but her father was in the diplomatic core so she grew up all around the world.'

'Is her husband coming too?' Esther asked.

'I'm not sure.' Carly frowned. 'It didn't sound like it but I didn't specifically ask that. I was too excited. I said I'll call her tomorrow so I'll get some more details.'

'It will be so good to see her again. I hope she can stay for a while.' Chloe missed having all four of them together. They had been such a tight unit and it had been hard to get used to being one friend short.

'And I hope she makes it in time for some of the pre-wedding celebrations,' Carly said.

'If she misses too many we'll just have to have more.' Esther laughed.

'That's our cue, gentlemen,' Harry interrupted. 'I feel wedding talk coming on. Let's organise some drinks.'

'A G&T?' Xander asked Chloe.

'Thanks.' She smiled. 'Are you okay with the men?'

'No worries.' He winked at her. 'Ladies.' He nodded towards Esther and Carly as he excused himself.

'Oh, my,' Carly said with a wicked grin as she fanned herself with her hand. 'He's seriously sexy. If only I wasn't engaged.'

'And pregnant,' Esther said.

'Maybe I can blame those pregnancy hormones.'

Chloe looked at Xander. He was wearing dark indigo jeans, black Australian stockman's boots and a plain grey T-shirt. A simple enough outfit, but when the T-shirt hugged his chest and hinted at the taut abdominals she'd glimpsed earlier and his jeans showcased his firm behind and the whole outfit was further highlighted by his blond Norse-god features she had to agree he looked good.

In Xander's case it wasn't so much the

clothes making the man as the man making the clothes.

'You never said he was Australian,' Esther said.

'Didn't I?'

'No. You didn't. You said he was from Wales.'

'I might have said he came here from Wales.'

'What else haven't you told us?'

'What do you mean?'

'You seem very comfortable together considering you've only just met—' Carly paused when Xander returned with Chloe's drink and turned to question him instead. 'You're Australian?'

'You're not going to hold that against me, are you? I have an English grandmother if that helps.'

'And you're here working with the air ambulance?'

'I'm on a sort of sabbatical.'

'A sabbatical?'

Xander nodded. 'I've been in Wales, Canada and South Africa working with their first response teams, their air ambulance services, which is their version of our flying doctor.'

'You're a flying doctor?'

'I am.'

'That job sounds amazing. The outback sounds so romantic.' Carly sighed.

'Is it like the movies, full of gorgeous men?' Esther wanted to know.

'Who ride horses and wrestle crocodiles?' Chloe laughed. 'Don't believe everything you see in the movies. There weren't that many gorgeous men.'

'Hey, I'm right here and I can hear you,' Xander protested. 'Should I be offended?' he asked, but he was smiling, clearly not offended.

'No, there were a few exceptions.' Chloe smiled back at him. His smile was impossible for her to resist. 'You were one.' She put her hand on his arm. It was a reflex and when she realised what she'd done she got flustered but she couldn't take it back, not immediately— that would just draw everyone's attention.

'Thank you.' Xander grinned and then answered Esther. 'Chloe's right, it's not exactly like the movies. Nothing ever is. But the landscape can be incredible if you can ignore the heat and the dust and the flies.'

'It must be exciting though? Flying around the country saving lives.'

'It's not like the air ambulance, it's not all emergencies. It can be routine. We do a lot of clinic runs, normal general practice type work.'

'Chloe did a study exchange with the flying doctor, didn't you, Chloe?' Esther said. 'The two of you didn't happen to meet while she was there?'

'We did. In Broken Hill.'

'Is that where you grew up?'

'No. I'm a city boy. But I love the flying doctor work. I'll be back in Adelaide when I go home.'

'When is that?'

'Soon, I think. I'm starting to miss the sun and the space. It's nearly time to go home.'

He looked at Chloe and she grew nervous. Not about him going but she knew she'd miss him. It would take her some time to adjust again to him not being part of her life.

But that wasn't going to be the case this time, was it? It was likely that he would be, if not a part of her life, of Lily's. She really did need to have those conversations. She needed to start making plans and she needed to know his position before she could move forward.

'Xander!' Harry called to him from the other side of the room. 'How are you at pool? We need a fourth.'

'What are the stakes?' he asked before he raised one eyebrow and winked at Chloe.

'Don't embarrass them,' she said. She recalled one evening around the billiard table in the Palace Hotel in Broken Hill when Xander had thoroughly trounced all challengers.

'I promise to miss a few,' he told her before excusing himself.

'You already knew him!' Carly accused Chloe once Xander had left them to join the men.

'The question is how well?' Esther said.

'Pretty well, judging by the heat between you,' Carly added.

'What do you mean?'

'He looks at you like it's Christmas Eve and you're his present under the tree, just waiting to be unwrapped.'

'And you kept touching his arm and every time you did he'd look at you like he just wanted to throw you over his shoulder and carry you out of here.'

'My God, Carly, your hormones really are addling your senses. Not everything is about sex.'

'I think Xander might disagree with me there.' Carly laughed. 'The sparks were flying.'

'There's something familiar about him.' Esther was looking at him.

'Stop staring!' Chloe hissed.

'Oh, my God.'

'What?'

'It's his eyes.'

Chloe panicked. 'Esther! Stop!' She hadn't even *considered* that her girlfriends would figure it out. She couldn't believe she'd been so stupid. Even if they hadn't put two and two together what if they'd said something about Lily in front of Xander?

'What is it?' Carly repeated.

'I've just figured it out.'

Chloe interrupted. She knew she had to say something and at least if she admitted the truth she could choose the decibel level. She was about to admit to something she did not want the whole world to hear. At least not yet.

'You have to promise me you won't say anything.' She eyeballed her girlfriends and waited until they kept quiet and nodded.

'Xander is Lily's father,' Chloe admitted in a whisper.

'He's your mystery man? Your wild weekend of hot Australian sex was with Xander?'

'Keep your voice down, Carly!'

Chloe had never pretended she didn't know who Lily's father was; she'd just chosen not to share the information. She'd told her girlfriends she'd had a brief fling and had never expected it to have any consequences.

'Wow.' Esther was looking in Xander's direction. 'Lily's father.'

'You can't say anything,' Chloe insisted. 'He doesn't know.'

'What do you mean he doesn't know?'

'I tried to find him when I found out I was pregnant but he'd left the flying doctor service and no one would tell me where he'd gone. Our relationship hadn't been serious—we hadn't made any promises about keeping in touch when I left. It was simply a holiday romance.'

'I thought you said it was one weekend?'

'It was a bit longer than a weekend,' she admitted now.

'How much longer?'

'Four weeks.'

'That sounds a bit more serious than a couple of nights?'

'It was never serious.' It wasn't *meant* to be serious but it couldn't be helped that she'd fallen for him anyway.

'Is that why you've never told us who Lily's father is? Because it wasn't serious?'

'No. Because I couldn't find him and I didn't think I should tell the world until I'd told him.'

'But you still haven't told him.'

She shook her head. 'I was waiting for the right time.'

'I don't think there is such a thing when the news is as big as this.'

'I know.' Chloe sighed. She had no choice now; she would definitely have to tell him tonight. It was going to be impossible to keep Lily a secret any longer. 'I've already decided I need to tell him tonight. I nearly mentioned Lily twice before we got here. I can't keep her a secret.'

Carly clapped her hands together. 'This is fabulous. You'll get your happily ever after as well.'

'I don't know about that. I have no idea how he feels about fatherhood, commitment, any of those things. He might want nothing to do with Lily. Or me.' Despite the brief conversations where he'd implied he wanted those things Chloe knew that talking the talk was very different to discovering that he was already a father.

'The way he was looking at you just before I don't think you have any worries there,' Carly said.

'You make such a cute couple,' Esther added. 'I'm going to invite him to my wedding.'

'You don't need to do that! I'm not even sure if he'll still be in London.'

'We'll see. I want things to work out for you.'

'I get that and I appreciate it. I'd like things

to work out for me too.' But she still wasn't sure exactly what that would look like.

Xander lined up the number thirteen ball, sinking it into the corner pocket. He missed his next shot but he and Adem only had two balls left to pot compared to Harry and Raphael's five, before they would win their second game. He stepped back, allowing Raphael to take his turn.

'Chloe tells me you and Carly are expecting a baby,' he said to Adem as he watched Raphael's ball hit the cushion and ricochet away from the pocket.

'Yes. I'm getting used to the idea,' he replied as Raphael's ball spun away and dropped into a pocket on the opposite side of the table. A lucky shot.

'It wasn't planned?'

'No. It was definitely a surprise but it's turned out to be a good one.'

Xander had always been slightly envious both of people who had children and of those for whom it happened so easily. His own plans for a family had derailed six years ago and he wondered now if he'd missed his opportunity.

Adem lined up to take his shot after Raphael missed the next ball. 'Have you got kids?' he asked.

'No.'

'Pity. I could use some advice,' Adem replied as the twelve ball dropped into a pocket.

'Don't you deal with babies all the time? You're an obstetrician, aren't you?'

'No, not me. Rafe is the obstetrician. I'm a neurosurgeon. I'm completely clueless when it comes to kids.' He potted the black ball, ending the game. 'Drinks on you,' he said to Harry and Raphael as they shook hands. 'Carly tells me we should be ready to be completely out of our depths, which I must say I don't find very reassuring,' he said as Raphael and Harry headed to the bar. 'I guess we'll be asking Chloe for a lot of advice.'

'Chloe? Why Chloe?' Xander wasn't following.

'She's the only one who's done this before.'

'What do you mean?'

'She's got a daughter.'

Xander's jaw fell open and he could feel the surprise written in his expression.

'You didn't know?' Adem asked.

Xander shook his head. He was at a complete loss, unable to think straight. He was glad the game was over. His head was full of white noise. Adem sounded as though he was talking under water.

Xander could feel himself sweating but he felt hot and cold at the same time.

'How old is she? The daughter.'

'I'm not sure. Little. Maybe two?'

Somehow he managed to get through one more drink before he escaped. He knew he was behaving badly but his head was reeling and he couldn't continue to stand at the bar and make polite conversation. He had to leave.

He ducked into the men's toilets and, from there, headed home. He didn't say goodnight to anyone. He sent Chloe a brief text with an excuse he suspected wouldn't hold up under examination but he couldn't think of anything substantial. He imagined she'd be upset but so was he. He'd deal with any repercussions of his early departure later. Right now he had other things on his mind.

Starting with, why hadn't Chloe said anything to him about her daughter? Lord knows, she'd had plenty of opportunity. Just a couple of hours ago they were talking about her experience with babies and she *still* didn't mention she had one of her own.

Why not?

It was only in hindsight as he marched along the footpath, constantly dodging and weaving to avoid other pedestrians—why couldn't these people stay out of his way?—

that he realised he should have asked Adem some questions. Any information might have been useful.

He wondered who the father was. *Where* the father was? Was he still involved with Chloe?

Of course he'd have to be. They had a child together.

Did this complicate things between them?

He suspected it would. It changed the dynamics of getting to know her again. She was part of a package now.

Was that something he was prepared for?

He didn't know. It was certainly not something he'd anticipated having to deal with.

Was that why she'd been quiet, introspective? Had she been worried he would find out? Concerned about what he'd think? How he'd feel? What he'd say?

She had reason to be, although at this stage he wasn't entirely sure how he felt.

He knew he didn't want to think of her with another man. He didn't want to think that she would be tied to someone else for ever through a child. That connection would continue and there was no way he could compete with that.

He realised then that he wanted to at least have a chance, an opportunity, to be important to Chloe. To pursue a relationship with her.

But now he would have to get in line. Behind a child. Behind an ex.

He needed time to think. About how he felt. About what this meant.

He had always wanted kids of his own. But did he want someone else's?

It wasn't a deal breaker, not with Chloe, but he did wish she'd told him. He wished he hadn't heard the news from a third party.

Why hadn't she said anything?

He'd turned the key in his front door and stepped inside. He pulled his boots off and stripped off his clothes, thinking of the high hopes he'd had for this evening when he'd got dressed just a few hours ago. This had not been how he'd thought his night would end.

He'd sleep on it, he decided, even though he suspected sleep might elude him, and ask her about it tomorrow.

CHAPTER SEVEN

Something's come up.

CHLOE DROPPED HER phone on the kitchen table after checking it for the tenth time since dropping Lily off at nursery that morning. But Xander's message from the night before still made no sense and she'd heard nothing further. She'd phoned him three times before giving up. He was either very busy or ignoring her calls. Given that he wasn't part of the overnight air ambulance team and he had no family in England that she knew of she couldn't imagine what had 'come up' and had required his immediate attention. Which really only left one possibility. That he was ignoring her.

She was annoyed that he'd disappeared last night without a decent explanation and was also slightly concerned that something had happened but there was nothing she could do about it at the moment. He would be back at work now, and while she could call the department, what would she say? He didn't really owe her anything. She just had to hope that he'd get in touch eventually and meanwhile she had plenty to keep her occupied for the morning while she waited. It was just unfortunate that it was only household chores.

She sighed as she dumped a load of wet laundry into a washing basket. There was no point trying to guess why he'd left. She'd drive herself mad. She just had to assume he had a reason and he'd explain it to her when she next saw him.

She was hanging the last item of washing on the line when she heard a siren wailing in the distance. It got louder. It was joined by another. A third. A fourth. She could hear ambulances, fire engines and police cars. Their different sirens colliding with each other at an ever-increasing volume.

She paused, resting the empty washing basket on her hip. Could she smell smoke?

She turned around in a circle, her face tilted up to the sky. There was a column of smoke to the west.

She hurried inside, dropping the basket on the floor as she flicked on the radio and the television, searching for news.

It didn't take long to hear. There was a fire

in a shopping centre. She knew the centre. It was only a few streets away.

It was a sprawling building with a supermarket as an anchor tenant, a gym, numerous restaurants, cafés and smaller speciality stores. It was a busy centre and Chloe knew it would have been bustling at ten o'clock in the morning. She could imagine the chaos of the evacuation.

She listened to the report. The origin of the fire was thought to be a café. The cause of the blaze as yet unknown. The list of casualties undetermined. The fire brigade, police and paramedics were all in attendance. Chloe's throat tightened in fear. Xander and both her brothers were working today. Were they there?

Her heart was pounding as she ran back outside. The column of smoke was thicker now, menacing and black. It was spreading across the sky. She heard the familiar sound of chopper blades and saw a news helicopter flying overhead. Followed by the air ambulance.

Xander.

She grabbed her keys and her phone and left the house. She sprinted west along the footpath. She knew there would be a crowd—disaster scenes were a magnet for the curious—but perhaps she could help.

She turned the final corner and was confronted by a wall of people. The noise was deafening—sirens, flames and voices all seemed to be at full volume. Soot fell from the sky and smoke was thick in the air. Chloe's eyes were stinging and her throat was dry.

Through the crowd she could see dozens of emergency vehicles filling the street. Police cars and ambulances but mostly fire engines.

The police were trying to clear the area of spectators, advising them to leave, but no one appeared to be listening. They held back the crowds but Chloe pushed her way through. She slid past some and ducked around others until she was close to the front. She looked for familiar faces. Guy. Tom. Xander. There were way too many paramedics and firefighters. She wasn't going to be able to identify her brothers so she looked instead for the orange jumpsuits of the air ambulance crew.

People were still running from the building, hurrying to escape, to get clear. It was pandemonium with the first responders doing their best to evacuate the building and get people triaged and treated. She wanted to offer to help but she knew she couldn't just speak to the first person she saw. Everyone was busy. No one had time to stop to talk to her.

If she wanted to help she needed to speak to whoever was in charge of coordinating the units, although it was difficult to tell who that might be. She doubted she'd be allowed to help. She wasn't on duty and she had no identification with her, but she had to do something.

She scanned the area but the crowds of people, the poor visibility due to the smoke and the incessant noise made it hard to pick out who was in charge. She needed to be up close to make herself heard. She didn't want to yell and add to the noise of the fire and of the emergency crews. The victims of the fire seemed mostly silent. In shock. A few were calling out, a few were in tears, but most were mute.

Chloe jumped as an explosion rent the air, adding to the noise and confusion. She turned back towards the building and saw a ball of flame shoot into the sky. A gas pipe must have exploded.

Movement on the periphery of her vision caught her eye. A woman, dazed and disoriented, was heading for the complex, heading back towards the fire, but it was the flash of orange that captured her attention. Someone was running towards the woman. Someone in an orange jumpsuit.

Xander.

He reached the woman just as Chloe thought

she couldn't get any closer to the fire without being burnt. Her heart was in her mouth as Xander reached out his hand to stop her from walking any further. They were only metres from the burning building.

A second explosion ripped through the air, tearing a massive hole in the side of the building.

Xander was in the path of the explosion.

Glass and bricks rained down on him. Chloe heard herself screaming a warning but of course he couldn't hear her. He disappeared in a cloud of dust and debris.

The dust cleared and Chloe could see him on the ground. He was lying over the woman, shielding her with his body, surrounded by flaming rubble.

Chloe waited for him to get up.

He didn't move.

Fire hoses were aimed at Xander and the woman. Showering them with water, dousing the flames.

He still didn't move.

Chloe tried desperately to push through the last row of people blocking her path but they were too tightly packed. She was stuck but she knew the police would stop her from reaching Xander even if she could get through the crowd. She peered over shoulders and saw paramedics hurrying towards them. One of them knelt beside Xander. She was sure it was Tom.

She watched as Xander was lifted onto a stretcher, an oxygen mask strapped over his face. Tom raised the stretcher and moved away from the building.

Chloe pushed back through the spectators, not towards the fire, not towards the police, but behind the crowd. She moved parallel to Tom, heading for the ambulances. Her eyes tracked Tom's movements and she was able to occasionally make him out between the heads of the onlookers.

He was almost at the ambulance. She picked up her pace; she needed to get to him before he left the scene. She drew level with the ambulance and pushed her way to the front again.

'*Tom.*' She called to him but he couldn't hear her.

'Tom!' she yelled again as she got past the crowd.

'You can't come through here.' A police-woman barred her way.

'Tom!' She was getting desperate.

Finally, Tom heard her and she saw him turn in her direction.

'Tom. That's Xander.' Her voice was hoarse.

Her throat was sore from screaming and her face was wet with tears she hadn't been aware of.

She saw Tom look to the stretcher where Xander lay and then back to her.

'It's okay. She's with the air ambulance.' He called out to the policewoman. 'Let her through.'

Chloe didn't give the policewoman time to argue. She ran to Tom. To Xander. All her earlier irritation over his disappearance last night forgotten. All she felt now was concern.

She put her hand on Xander's leg. His eyes were closed. His blond hair dirty with soot and ash. 'Xander? Can you hear me?'

There was no reply.

'Is he breathing?' she asked her brother, even as she realised he must be. They weren't trying to resuscitate him. He had an oxygen mask over his nose and mouth.

'Yes,' Tom said as he pushed the stretcher into the ambulance, 'but he's non-responsive.'

Xander's uniform was scorched. It was flame retardant but hadn't completely withstood the direct heat. She could see marks on his neck and wrists. Were they burns or just dirt? How badly was he injured?

Chloe put her hand on Tom's arm, stopping

him from climbing into the ambulance. 'Can I come with you?'

He nodded. 'Ride in the front with Diane. There's no room in the back.'

Chloe didn't want to leave Xander but she didn't argue. She jumped into the front of the ambulance as Diane slammed the rear doors shut before climbing into the driver's seat.

'Where are we headed?' Chloe asked.

'St Barbara's Hospital.'

'But the Queen Victoria is closer,' she argued.

'I know,' Diane said. 'But the category one cases are being sent there. The less urgent ones have been directed to other hospitals.'

Chloe bit back a cry of frustration. She knew it wasn't Diane's fault but if they'd been able to go to the Queen Victoria Chloe would have some influence. She tried to console herself with the knowledge that they didn't think Xander was critically injured.

Chloe was out of the ambulance almost before Diane had pulled to a stop in the emergency bay of St Barbara's. She waited impatiently for Diane to open the rear doors as it wasn't Chloe's job, and once they got inside she wouldn't have a job to do either. It wasn't her hospital. She'd be helpless, useless. She'd have nothing to do except wait.

Diane and Tom pulled Xander's stretcher out. He still hadn't regained consciousness.

They pushed him inside. The hospital was busy but Xander was given priority. His airway, lungs and other injuries needed urgent assessment. He was whisked away and she knew she wouldn't be allowed to go with him. She would have to wait.

She had never been on the other side of an Accident and Emergency department. She'd never been one of the anxious family or friends waiting for news.

She wished she knew someone on staff but she had to sit and wait like everyone else. The television in the waiting area had been tuned into the news channel, which was still showing footage of the burning building. Chloe knew there would be fatalities.

She was worried about her brothers. Tom had gone back to the scene and she knew Guy would still be there too.

She was worried about Xander.

She didn't want to harass the staff. She knew what it was like to have patients' relatives asking for updates every few minutes, but the delay seemed interminable. She had to know if he was all right. She had to see him.

She waited as long as she could bear before approaching the unit manager. 'Can you tell me if there's any news on Xander Jameson. He was brought in from the fire.'

'Are you family?'

'No. I'm a friend and a midwife at the Queen Victoria. I work with Xander at the air ambulance.'

'Do you have some ID?'

She shook her head. She'd dashed out of the house with only her keys and her phone. She hadn't thought to grab her bag or her wallet.

'Then I'll have to ask you to wait.'

Chloe was prepared to wait. She'd known it was unlikely that she'd be given any information just on her say-so but she wasn't leaving until she had some news. She would wait until Xander could vouch for her. 'Can you ask him if I can see him?' she said as she took a seat.

'When I can.'

Chloe had no idea if that meant Xander had regained consciousness and the manager would ask when she had a minute or if it meant Xander was still out cold.

She nodded. She couldn't complain. She knew there was a protocol to follow and she didn't want to cause a scene.

But what if something serious had happened to him?

What if she lost him all over again?

Why had she been hesitating to talk to him? To tell him what had happened. She should have told him about Lily. She should have told him how she felt. He deserved to know the truth.

'You have a visitor.'

Xander turned his head to look at the nurse and winced as pain shot behind one eye.

'Who is it?' he asked. He couldn't imagine too many people who would be visiting him.

'I don't know,' she replied. 'Shall I ask?' The nurse was young, a student, and she looked nervous. Xander assumed she was aware he was a doctor and that was putting her on edge.

That would probably be a good idea, he felt like saying, but it wouldn't serve any purpose to snap at her. He was still groggy. And sore. He'd been surprised to find himself in hospital. He remembered chasing after a woman at the fire but had no memory of anything after that.

'Male or female?' he asked.

'Female.'

'What does she look like?'

'Young. Blond curly hair. She said she's a midwife.'

Chloe.

'You can send her in.'

Chloe came into his room. Her face was pale, her normal happy expression overshadowed by a crease between her brows. She looked worried.

She came straight to his bed but hesitated a step away. She stopped and he wondered what she'd wanted to do. 'You're okay?' she said.

He nodded. 'Is the fire out?'

Chloe shook her head. 'What were you thinking?' She sounded cross. 'Running after that woman.'

He hadn't been thinking; he'd simply reacted when he saw the woman heading towards the fire. 'Is she okay?'

'I don't know. I think so. You know that going into burning buildings isn't your job.'

'I didn't go inside,' he argued. 'She was walking straight into the fire. Someone had to stop her and there was no one else nearby.'

'But you could have been killed!'

Was she worried about *him*? Afraid for his safety? Afraid that he had been injured?

He didn't want her to worry about him. 'I'm sorry if I scared you,' he said, hoping to reassure her. 'But, as you can see, I'm fine.'

'Are you sure?'

'I'm positive.'

'You were knocked unconscious,' she argued.

'Only briefly.' He tried a self-deprecating smile for good measure.

'Promise you won't do that again.'

'I'll try not to make a habit of it.'

She smiled and he saw her shoulders visibly relax.

She reached out and held his fingers. 'What happened to your arm?'

His left arm was wrapped in gauze bandages. 'The doctors picked some glass fragments out. They've cleaned and dressed it. That's all. Nothing major.'

She put her hand to his chin and turned his head slightly. 'And what about this?' she asked.

He had a dressing on his neck and he felt it pull tight, resisting the movement. He tried not to wince. 'A minor burn.'

He had a dull headache and suspected he had sustained a mild concussion but he expected the pain relief would take care of the ache. There was something niggling at the back of his mind and he concentrated hard to bring it to the forefront. He felt it was important. Something to do with Chloe.

A conversation.

He closed his eyes as the memory returned.

A conversation not with Chloe but with Adem.

'Are you all right? Can I get you something?' Chloe's voice broke into his reverie.

He opened his eyes. 'I'm fine,' he reiterated as he fought down a wave of nausea. He knew he wasn't physically sick. It was emotional. 'But there's something I need to ask you.'

Now that he'd remembered the conversation, he knew it would eat away at him until he raised the subject with Chloe. He was tired and sore but he needed some answers. They needed to have a conversation and while the emergency department wasn't the ideal place it would have to do. The sooner he heard her side of the story, the sooner he would know where he stood.

'Adem told me you have a daughter.'

The colour that had been beginning to return to her face drained away completely, leaving her ashen. She froze.

'When did he tell you that?'

'Last night. At the bar.'

'That's why you left,' she said as she collapsed onto the chair next to his bed.

'Is it true?'

She nodded.

'Why haven't you said anything?'

'I was waiting for the right time.'

'We were talking about your nephew, about babies, just yesterday. Why didn't you tell me then?'

'Are you upset?'

'Damn right I am.' Her brown eyes were wide, worried, but he wasn't going to pretend everything was fine. 'I'm upset that you haven't shared this with me. We were talking about what you've been doing for the past four years. You told me about your plan to work for the air ambulance. You didn't think to mention you'd had a baby in that time?'

'Are you angry?'

'Angry? No.' He was but he couldn't share that he was mostly jealous that she had this history, a child, with someone who wasn't him. He thought that would make him sound petty. 'I'm frustrated that you kept this from me. That you didn't trust me.'

'It wasn't that I didn't trust you. I didn't know how you'd feel but I was going to tell you about her last night. I had planned to tell you after drinks but you'd already left.'

'That's a convenient story.'

'It's the truth. I'm sorry. I should have told you about her. You should meet her.'

She looked close to tears and Xander moderated his tone. He didn't want to argue. He didn't have the energy. 'I'm not saying I have to meet her. I just wish you'd mentioned her.'

'I think you should meet her. Lily has just turned three.' Chloe was looking at him as if she expected him to say something. His head was hurting and he couldn't figure out what response she expected him to make. In his silence, she continued. 'She's your daughter.'

CHAPTER EIGHT

XANDER FELT THE world stop.

'What did you say?'

'Lily is your daughter. You're her father.'

He shook his head as the nausea burnt his oesophagus. 'She can't be mine.'

An alarm was beeping.

He had forgotten that he was connected to monitors and the rapid acceleration of his heart rate triggered a warning. The young nurse came back into his room.

'Is everything all right? Do you need to rest?'

'No. I'm fine. Just switch the damn machine off.'

He saw the young girl glance at Chloe and he wondered if she was going to ask Chloe to leave but she just raised an eyebrow and Chloe nodded once, as if giving her permission to do as Xander said. She didn't need Chloe's permission but Xander knew he'd frightened her, given her a story to tell about how doctors made terrible patients, but he didn't care. The nurse pressed some buttons, resetting the machine, and scurried off.

He stared at Chloe. Waiting for her to speak. Waiting for the truth.

'I promise you, Lily is your child.'

There was no way Chloe was telling the truth but she couldn't know how her words pierced his heart. She couldn't know how he'd wished for a child but knew that wish would be denied him.

There had to be another explanation. He'd known last night that another man had fathered a child with Chloe and he knew that was still the case today. There was another man somewhere in this story.

The question was—who was that man, because he was certain it wasn't him.

'She can't be mine,' he repeated.

Chloe listened to Xander repeat his words. Did he think that the more he said it, the truer it would become? Did he think she'd change her mind in the face of his denial?

It was her turn now to be frustrated.

She was annoyed with herself. She hadn't anticipated the conversation happening like this at all. She'd thought she'd be able to control it. To direct the conversation. To break the news to him gently.

She should have realised he wouldn't believe her. She remembered his reaction to Hannah and Guy's situation. He'd felt Hannah was tricking Guy. She should have expected this reaction but she'd been lulled into a false sense of security by Guy and Hannah's experience. They trusted one another but she and Xander didn't have that same level of trust. She wished they did but she knew that required a strong foundation to a relationship and she wasn't even sure they *had* a relationship.

She'd handled it badly but she wasn't expecting to have to defend herself.

She needed to stay calm. She needed to see things from his perspective.

No one deserved to find out about parenthood this way. He was experiencing the same shock that Hannah and Guy must have felt and she'd empathised with them over that.

She closed her eyes and counted to ten.

But Xander wasn't giving her any leeway.

'You've made a mistake, Chloe,' he continued. 'I'm not her father.'

'Why not?'

'Because I can't have children.'

'What? Why would you say that? Are you accusing me of lying?'

'No. I'm saying you've made a mistake.'

'Why would you think that? I know how a pregnancy happens.'

'There must be someone else.'

'There was no one else.' Her voice was tight with anger and she fought hard to try to keep her tone level. 'I know how a pregnancy happens and I know how long it lasts. I *know* who I was sleeping with when I fell pregnant and that was you.'

'It can't have been me.'

'I promise you. It was.'

'Chloe, I can't have children.'

'Why would you say that? Lily is your daughter.'

'She can't be. I can't have children,' he repeated. 'That's why my wife left me.'

'What?' She didn't understand what he was telling her. She *knew* Lily was his. There was no doubt about that.

'My wife, ex-wife, wanted to have children. We tried naturally and when nothing happened we tried IVF. We had four cycles.'

'Four? And then you gave up? Surely that's not enough attempts to decide you can't have kids.'

'We gave up because, in the middle of all

of that, my wife had an affair. That's why we split up.'

'But if you'd kept going you might have been successful. Maybe it was a problem with your wife? Sometimes a different partner makes a difference.'

'The problem was with me,' he said. His grey eyes were dark as he asked, 'If you think I'm the father why didn't you tell me you were pregnant when you found out?'

'I didn't know I was pregnant until after I got home. I tried to find you but you'd disappeared. I got in touch with the flying doctor service in Broken Hill but I was told you weren't working there any more. I contacted the headquarters in Adelaide but HR wouldn't pass on your information. No one would tell me anything and I started to wonder if you'd instructed them not to pass on your details. If you thought I'd become a crazy stalker.

'You weren't on social media,' she continued. 'I didn't know where you were living, where you'd gone. I called Jane, you remember Jane, the flight nurse, but she also said you'd left and she didn't know where you were. I couldn't afford to hire anyone to look for you and then, when Lily was born, I didn't have time to keep looking.'

'So instead you kept her a secret.'

'Not intentionally! I tried to find you.'

'Why didn't you send a letter to the flying doctor base and ask them to forward it to me?'

'I did. I sent a letter by registered mail. I wanted you to sign for it. I wanted to make sure it got to you. I thought it was all too easy for the letter to get lost, or for you to say you never received it, especially if you didn't like what it said, and I would never know the truth, but it came back unopened.'

'Do you have any proof she's mine?'

'How could I? Won't you take my word for it?'

He shook his head, wincing with the movement. 'I can't.'

Chloe wondered whether she should show him photos of Lily on her phone. She had hundreds. But Lily looked so much like her that she doubted he'd be able to see any resemblance to himself in his current state of mind. Would he see himself in Lily's grey eyes?

Only if he wanted to.

'How old is she?' he asked.

'She turned three on the tenth of March. She was due in April but she was born six weeks premature. I was in Australia from May to July,' she said. 'I only slept with you. You do the maths.'

'It's not a question of maths. It's a question of probability.'

'Last time I checked, that was maths.'

Xander sighed and rubbed his head. Chloe felt slightly guilty that they were arguing about Lily while he was in his current state but she was upset too. This was not going the way she'd hoped but it was exactly what she'd been afraid of—not knowing how he would react.

It wasn't ideal having this conversation while he was sore, and medicated, and judging by the look of him, nursing a cracking headache but he'd raised the subject.

'I'm not sure that now is the right time to be having this discussion,' she said, knowing they hadn't finished but they both needed some time to calm down.

'You're right,' he replied. 'I think you should go.'

Xander stared out of the window of his rental accommodation. The sky outside was grey and heavy and the weather was dismal, like his mood. Five days after the fire, almost six since Adem had given him the news, and he still wasn't sure how he felt. He wanted to believe Chloe but how could it be true?

How could Chloe's daughter be his?

Could he really be a father?

He wanted it to be true but he knew the chances were slim. But why would she lie? What did she hope to gain from this? And if she was telling the truth, then he'd missed out on three years of his daughter's life. How could she do that to him?

His mind continued in a never-ending circle, hour upon hour, day after day.

When he'd confronted her about her child he'd assumed another man was the father. He'd anticipated feeling self-righteous, upset that she hadn't shared her story with him. He hadn't expected it to become *his* story.

In the five days since the fire he was no closer to figuring it out. He had taken sick leave from the air ambulance but was due back at work tomorrow. He had used the downtime to do some things he should have done years ago. He'd called in some favours. Had some tests.

He scrolled through his emails, looking for the one he had forwarded to his oncologist in Australia. He checked the time and read through the scanned report as he waited for a phone call.

His phone vibrated on the table and the sudden noise in the silence of the room startled him. His hands shook with nerves as he read the number on the screen. An international code. He hesitated before accepting the call. It was the one he'd been waiting for but now he wasn't sure if he was ready for an answer.

'You got my email?' he asked, barely managing to get the pleasantries out of the way first. 'Is it possible for me to have children?'

'Yes, is the short answer. Your sperm count and motility is normal. On the low side of normal, which means you'd probably have more chance of having children with a young woman, but it's completely possible. Have you met someone?'

'Sort of.' How did he explain Chloe? 'There's a woman claiming I'm the father of her child,' he said, realising he didn't need to explain the situation more specifically than that.

'So your question is retrospective? You're not planning for the future?'

'No, this has already happened.'

'And you didn't know?'

'I've just found out.'

'How old is the child?'

'Three.'

'So, the pregnancy would have occurred almost four years ago?'

'Yes. Two years post-chemo,' Xander said.

'Your sperm could have recovered by then.

Did you not test a sample after you finished treatment?'

'No.' Xander shook his head. 'There wasn't any need. We had embryos frozen at the time I was diagnosed so I started treatment immediately and then Heather and I separated after the last lot of embryos failed to implant. After that it didn't matter to me. I wasn't worried about whether or not I could father children. It wasn't something I was thinking about at that point.'

'Without a comparison sample I can't tell you what the situation was four years ago. There's a chance that the child is yours but it would be a slight chance. DNA would be the only way to know for sure.'

Could it be true? Could he have a daughter?

Lily. He hung up the phone and said her name out loud for the first time.

Lily Jameson. It was a pretty name, although it was more likely to be Lily Larson.

Regardless of what her full name was or whether or not Lily was his he needed to apologise to Chloe. He'd handled the discussion badly, although he didn't feel he was completely to blame. She'd blindsided him. He knew he'd brought up the subject but if he'd anticipated how the conversation would go, he would have waited until the painkillers had worn off. Until his head, and his mind, were clear. And no matter what condition he was in, no matter that he had raised the topic, she'd had ample opportunity to tell him about this child, his child, before then and she hadn't. But still, he needed to clear the air.

Chloe was surprised to run into Xander when she walked out of the hospital. It was almost a week since the fire. Almost a week since she'd told him about Lily. Since he'd asked her to leave him be and she hadn't heard from him since. She'd been going crazy, running through different scenarios in her head, trying to guess what he was thinking. What he was planning.

He was leaning against the wall outside the A&E and he straightened up when he saw her and stepped forward. She knew he was waiting for her.

As she got closer she could see he was tired and his grey eyes were full of shadows.

'What are you doing here?'

'I thought we needed to talk.' He was holding a bunch of flowers and he held them out to her. 'These are for you. I owe you an apology.'

No one had ever given her flowers before, Chloe thought as she took them from him. It was an enormous bouquet of lilies. Had he chosen lilies deliberately? She was scared to ask him. Scared of what it might mean.

'Have you got time to take a walk with me?' he asked.

She nodded and fell into step beside him. She was pleased to have the lilies to hold. It gave her something to do with her hands and made her keep a little bit of distance from him. She needed to know what he wanted but she was terrified of what she might hear.

'I reacted badly,' he said, 'and I'm sorry. Your news took me by surprise, but still, I should have handled it better.'

'Are you saying you believe me now?'

'I'm still not sure.'

Chloe stopped in her tracks and turned to face him. 'What exactly are you saying, then? What exactly are you apologising for?'

'Let me explain.' He leant on the embankment railing and stared across the river, avoiding eye contact. 'I told you my wife and I got divorced because we couldn't conceive. That is true but it's not the whole truth. We'd tried for a year to conceive naturally and then started IVF. We'd gone through two cycles unsuccessfully when I was diagnosed with testicular cancer.'

'What?' She couldn't believe he'd dropped that into the conversation as if it was of no consequence. 'You had cancer? You accused *me* of keeping things from you. At least I *tried* to find you. I *tried* to tell you I was pregnant. Why didn't you tell me about the cancer?'

He shrugged. 'We didn't talk much about anything personal. And I was angry. There was a lot of stuff happening in my life when we met. I was grieving. I'd lost my marriage, my health and potentially my chance of having a family of my own. I was in a dark place and you were the one bright light, the one good thing, but you were fleeting. I didn't want to sully things by talking about what I'd been going through—it wasn't important when I was with you. You gave me a chance to focus on something else and I was grateful for that. You were the one thing that gave me hope that I would get through that period of time and come out the other side.'

Chloe thought back to when they'd met. She knew he'd been unhappy and she'd taken pleasure in the knowledge that she had been able to make him laugh and smile. That she'd been able to lift those shadows from his eyes even though it had only been temporary. She'd attributed his sadness to his divorce. She'd never imagined there was more to his despair. He was right—they hadn't talked much.

'Heather, my ex-wife, is a couple of years

older than me and her biological clock was working overtime. When I was diagnosed I wanted to start chemotherapy immediately. We had some frozen embryos in reserve so we continued with IVF while I started treatment. I assumed we'd get lucky with IVF—after all, how much bad luck can two people have—but when none of those embryos implanted successfully either Heather started to consider her options.

'I was told it could take two years before my sperm was viable again and, worst case, it may never recover. I guess Heather figured I was a bad bet and she couldn't wait—she didn't *want* to wait—for me to recover. I never really found out where her head was at. We were both stressed for different reasons.

'I foolishly expected her to stick by me, for better or worse. She could only see the worse. She had an affair and fell pregnant. I still wonder if it was deliberate. It was one way to make sure I'd let her go. Loyalty and honesty are really important to me and she betrayed me. Betrayed my trust.

'So yes, when I met you I was angry and the last thing I wanted to talk about was my divorce or my diagnosis because they were interrelated. One had led to the other and I really just wanted to pretend none of it had happened. Heather had just remarried. She'd wanted to make things official with her new partner before the baby was born so I agreed to the divorce. My whole life had come crashing down and I was living one day at a time. I was too scared to look too far into the future. I didn't know what sort of future I was going to have.'

'That's a lot to get my head around.'

'I know. Can you understand why I didn't want to talk about it four years ago? I just needed to forget.'

Chloe nodded. She could understand. But that didn't mean she had to like it. 'How long ago were you diagnosed?'

'Six years.'

'Are you okay now?'

'I'd say I'm fine.'

'*You'd* say. What do your specialists say?'

'That I'm cancer-free.'

'Did you have a sperm count done after you finished chemo?'

'No.'

'So you don't *know* that you can't have children.'

'No. Not definitively.'

She withdrew her phone and turned it on, opening her photos. She held it out to him.

'This is Lily. She has your eyes.' She'd

taken it yesterday, deliberately making sure she got Lily's eyes to their best advantage. 'I'd like you to meet her. Do you think that's something you could do?'

He nodded but without any excitement. Without any anticipation. His eyes were dark with shadows back and she knew she'd put them there. She wanted the other Xander back, the one who looked like he wanted to love her. She wondered if he was gone for good.

CHAPTER NINE

XANDER WAS NERVOUS when he knocked on Chloe's door. He had agreed to meet her at her house. She'd felt Lily would be more comfortable in a familiar environment and he hadn't argued. It wasn't every day you got to meet a potential offspring and he wanted to make a good impression. He wanted Lily to like him.

He wiped his palms over the seat of his jeans, making sure they weren't clammy.

'Hi.' Chloe was smiling when she opened the door. She was wearing a pink T-shirt with cut-off denim shorts and canvas trainers. She looked good, she looked relaxed, and Xander felt some of his nervous tension dissipate.

'Hi.'

'I thought we'd take Lily to the park. She's learning to ride her bike—it will be better for all of us if she has an activity to focus on. Is that okay?'

'Of course.'

'Great. I'll get her. Do you want to wait here?'

She left him on the doorstep and his nerves returned.

'Lily, this is my friend from work, Xander. Xander, this is Lily.'

They were back.

He looked down into a face that was a miniature version of Chloe's, albeit with strawberry blond curls and grey eyes.

Chloe was right. She did have his eyes.

He tried not to stare.

Could she really be his?

'Hello, Lily.'

'Hello.'

'Xander is a doctor. He works in the helicopter.'

'Do you fly the helichopper?' she asked, and her expression was so like one of his sister's that it made him do a double take. She was definitely a Jameson around the eyes but the rest of her was Chloe.

He shook his head. 'No. That's Simon's job.'

'Uncle Tom drives an ambliance and Uncle Guy drives a fire engine.'

'That sounds very exciting.'

'Uncle Guy took me in the fire engine. Do you want to see my bike? Uncle Guy bought it for me.'

'I'd love to see your bike.'

Xander walked behind Lily and watched her wobble along on her bike as Chloe occasionally gave her a little push to get her moving or a steadying hand to keep her balance. His heart swelled with pride at the idea that this gorgeous, bubbly little girl could be his.

His daughter.

But that in itself was a dilemma.

He was due to go home soon. But he knew he wouldn't leave if it meant leaving his daughter behind. There was no way he was going to give her up. He needed to get to know her. He needed her to know him. He couldn't believe he'd missed three years of her life already. He wasn't going to miss any more.

Chloe had explained that she'd tried to find him and he had to believe her. He knew he'd been virtually untraceable for the better part of four years. That had been what he'd wanted. To disappear. He couldn't blame Chloe. It was *his* fault his daughter didn't know him. But he couldn't help but wonder if Chloe could have tried harder.

He had a daughter.

Was she really his? Could it be true?

He didn't care if it wasn't, he realised. He wanted it to be true.

'Why didn't you try harder to find me?' he

asked as Lily rode ahead of them. 'Why didn't you try again?'

'I didn't stop completely. I searched the internet every year around Lily's birthday. I found a couple of articles about you on a Canadian website about a year ago but when I called the ambulance service there you had already moved on and once again the service wouldn't provide me with any details.' She shrugged. 'So I gave up again. I'm sorry. I don't know what else I could have done.'

'What have you told Lily about her father?' he asked as Lily abandoned her bicycle in favour of the slide.

'That he lives in Australia, which is a very long way away, but that he loves her very much. Now that we've found you I need to know if that is true before we tell her who you are. If you don't want to be a part of her life, I'm not going to tell her any more about you but when she is older I won't stop her from contacting you. What happens next is up to you.'

Lily was running towards them and Chloe stood up, wrapped up the conversation. 'We need to go home now. Lily needs her afternoon nap.'

Chloe sent Lily inside to wash her hands when they got home. And Xander knew it was time for him to take his leave. The Larson family had their lives to lead and he wasn't part of it yet.

Chloe handed him a large envelope as she walked with him to the front gate.

'What is this?'

'It's our DNA samples. Mine and Lily's.'

'You've done a test?' He was surprised.

Chloe nodded.

'Why?'

'I've thought about what you said and I decided your concerns were valid. I shouldn't have dismissed them. There was no reason for you to believe me, even without your history. The tests were non-invasive. Lily was quite happy to copy me when I did my cheek swab. It wasn't difficult and I thought it was only fair to you. I'm claiming that you are Lily's father and I'm happy to prove it to you. I know what the tests results will show. It's only fair that you have the confirmation you wanted.'

Xander took the envelope.

'And if you are free tomorrow,' Chloe said, 'I thought we could spend the day together again? Just the three of us?'

'I'd like that,' he said as he bent and kissed her on the cheek. He'd take whatever she offered him at the moment. She'd turned his world upside down but he had to hope it would be in a positive way.

'Where would you like to go first?' Chloe asked as she reversed her car into a parking space near the Brighton pier. The forecast was for a beautiful day and she had decided to take Xander out of the city and Brighton had numerous attractions that would keep Lily entertained and give them all a chance to spend some time together away from her family.

'What are the options?'

'The Pier, the aquarium, the beach, the Tower.'

'What would Lily like?'

'Probably the Pier.'

Xander had charmed everyone today when he'd met her family. He had the advantage—her family knew this situation was a shock for him and they were taking it easy on him. They hadn't bombarded him with questions; instead they were giving him time to slowly acclimatise to the idea of being a father and gaining an instant family in the Larsons. He'd handled it well, meeting everyone, but Chloe still didn't know how he was feeling about the instant fatherhood. Was he accepting the situation or was he still wary, unsure, uncertain?

She hoped he would do his DNA test soon.

She knew the results would corroborate her claims and, in her opinion, the sooner that happened, the better. They couldn't really move forward until Lily's parentage was confirmed and they needed to work out where they went from here. There were a lot of unknowns in this new situation she found herself in.

They walked past the Royal Pavilion as they made their way to the pier.

'A palace!' Lily cried. 'Is there a princess in there? Can we visit her? I'd like to be a princess,' she continued without pausing for breath. 'I'd like to live in a palace and wear pretty dresses every day.'

'Do all three-year-olds talk this much?' Xander wanted to know.

'She does have good language skills. I think it's because she spends so much time around adults. Me, my mum, my brothers. There's always someone to talk to or a conversation to listen in on. Her ears are almost as big as her vocabulary.'

'Who is your favourite princess, Lily?'

'Anna.'

Xander looked at Chloe and she knew he had no idea who Lily was talking about. She figured he would know the traditional fairy-tale princesses but Anna and her sister, Elsa, were far from traditional.

'Anna looks a bit like Lily,' she said, explaining the attraction.

Lily nodded and said, 'She has hair like mine.'

'Can you show me a picture on my phone?' Xander asked as he squatted down beside Lily and opened a browser on his phone.

He admired several photos of Anna, Elsa and even Olaf as they waited for their turn on the carousel and kept up a conversation with Lily, which was not an easy thing to do. She chattered non-stop and changed topics rapidly, making it difficult to keep up with her train of thought, but Xander seemed to take it all in his stride. Was he warming to the idea of being a father?

Chloe listened as Lily giggled in response to Xander's questions about the characters. He had an affinity with Lily. Did he feel a connection with her or was Chloe making more out of this than it really was? Was she hoping for more?

She knew she was.

'Can I go on the trampoline, Mummy?' Lily asked as Xander lifted her off the carousel horse at the end of the ride.

'Not yet, baby girl. You have to be a bit taller.'

Lily started to pout and Chloe expected an argument but Xander jumped in. 'I'll bring you back when you're taller, Lily, but why don't you choose something else for now.'

'You shouldn't make those promises,' Chloe said quietly. 'You might not be able to keep them.'

'I always keep my promises,' he insisted. 'I am a man of my word. Honesty and loyalty are really important to me.'

Chloe let it slide. She wasn't going to get into a debate about that in the middle of an amusement park.

'Which ride would you like, Lily?'

'I'll sit this one out,' Chloe said when Lily insisted on a turn on the spinning cups and saucers.

'Really? What happened to your adventurous spirit?'

Four years ago she had wanted to try everything in the outback. She'd been young, full of adventure and full of joy. Sometimes it seemed like a lifetime ago. 'I can't handle the spinning motion,' she said honestly as she handed over two tickets for the ride.

'Time for one last ride,' Chloe said as her

daughter and Xander climbed out of the cups. 'Which one would you like?'

'That one.' Lily pointed at a brightly lit ride that had miniature vehicles 'driving' around a track. Chloe could see an ambulance, a fire engine, a racing car and a rocket. 'I want to sit in the fire engine like Uncle Guy.'

Chloe stood at the barrier, watching Lily on the ride. She felt Xander stand behind her but when he put his hands on her hips she jumped at his touch. She hadn't been expecting that. He'd kissed her on the cheek yesterday, chaste, distracted, leaving her worried about what damage she'd done to their relationship. She wondered if the news about Lily had overshadowed their chemistry. Had it changed Xander's view of her, and of their relationship? Was it more serious? Different? Would Lily become his priority and would Chloe be pushed aside?

She didn't know where they were at. She had no idea how he was feeling.

'Is that okay?' he asked.

She hesitated.

It felt nice. She leant back into him, very slightly, and nodded. She actually wouldn't mind if he wrapped his arms around her but Lily would be sure to notice and would be bound to ask why. Most of her questions at the moment started with that word.

Xander stood behind Chloe and watched Lily. He had his hands on Chloe's hips but he'd felt her stiffen at his touch.

'Is that okay?' he asked, and then she relaxed into him. He was close enough to smell her hair. She smelt like shampoo and sunshine. He felt her apprehension, her worry, and he tried to reassure her. 'It will be all right,' he said. 'We'll figure it all out.'

He was feeling positive about the future. It had taken him a long time but he was certain things would work out. He didn't believe in coincidences but he believed in fate. In things that were meant to be.

'I'm hungry.' The ride had finished and Lily was standing in front of them again.

'How about we get some hot chips for lunch?' he suggested.

Lily clapped her hands. 'I love hot chippies.'

'So does your mum. Especially when they're somebody else's,' he said with a wink in Chloe's direction.

She laughed, as he'd intended her to, and said, 'They taste better off someone else's plate.'

'So I've noticed.'

They sat in the sunshine outside the fish and chip shop and watched as Lily threw almost as many chips to the seagulls as she ate. She climbed off the bench to chase the birds as Chloe cautioned her. 'Be careful, Lily.'

Xander was watching Lily and saw her trip and, almost in slow motion, fall and land awkwardly, her arms outstretched.

Chloe was up out of her seat but Xander was faster. Three strides and he was beside her.

He and Chloe knelt on the ground but the moment Chloe touched Lily, her daughter screamed.

'Hang on, Chloe, let me have a look at her.'

Lily was as white as a ghost and her left wrist was swelling already. She cradled it protectively against her body.

'Chloe. Look at me.' She was agitated and he waited for her to focus. 'I think she may have a greenstick fracture. She needs to go to hospital. Do you know where the closest one is?'

Chloe didn't answer and Xander realised she was in shock.

'Do you need some help?' A lady pushing a pram stopped beside them.

'Do you know if there's a hospital near here?' Xander asked.

'The children's hospital is about a mile from here,' she said as she pointed to their right.

'Chloe, give me your scarf. I'll immobilise her arm as best as I can.'

He wanted to be able to help. He wanted to be useful. He wound the scarf over one shoulder and behind Lily's back holding her arm against her chest to stop it from bouncing around as he explained what he was doing. 'We need to take you to the hospital. We're going to take a picture of your arm and see what you've done.'

He scooped her up in his arms and headed for the car.

Xander parked the car in a doctor's bay in front of the hospital. He didn't care for procedure. His priority was getting Lily into the A&E. He carried her inside as Chloe walked beside them. He spied a wheelchair just inside the door and gently lowered Lily into it as he heard someone exclaim.

'Chloe? What are you doing here?'

'Joanna!'

Xander looked up to see Chloe being greeted by a woman in a nurse's uniform. He listened while Chloe explained what had happened. She seemed to have recovered her wits. She was still pale but the shock seemed to have eased.

'I didn't know you worked here,' she was saying before she glanced his way. 'Xander is a doctor. He thinks she has a greenstick fracture of her wrist.'

Lily was still pale and teary but she sat silently in the chair.

Joanna glanced at her quickly and nodded. 'Give me a second and I'll organise an X-ray,' she said as she gathered some forms. 'Can you fill these out?'

Xander took the forms. 'I'll do it,' he said to Chloe. 'You go with Lily.'

Chloe didn't argue. She followed behind Joanna as she pushed Lily's wheelchair through the next set of doors, whisking her away and leaving Xander alone. He sat in the waiting room and read through the forms. He filled in Lily's birthday and her address but that was as much as he knew. There was no way he could complete the form without Chloe's help. He knew so little about the girl who was supposedly his daughter. He didn't know her middle name or even her surname. If she had allergies. He knew almost nothing about her and only a bit more about her mother. But he could feel himself being drawn in. He didn't want to let Chloe go. Not this time. Not again. She came as a package deal now but that was okay.

Joanna reappeared and Xander stood up, waiting for news.

'You were right. It looks like a greenstick fracture. I've left them in a treatment bay—they're just waiting for a doctor's consult. Have you finished with the forms?'

Xander shook his head. 'No. I need Chloe to fill out some of the detail.'

Joanna looked sideways at him, obviously assuming he was Lily's father and then assuming he was an idiot. He didn't correct her, on either assumption. 'Come with me, you can wait with them.'

She took him in to Chloe and Lily.

'I need your help with the forms,' Xander said to Chloe. 'I've got her birthday as March the tenth. Does she have a middle name?'

'Alexandra.'

'Alexandra?'

Chloe nodded. 'I wanted to give her something of yours. That was the closest I could manage.'

'Thank you.' It was an unexpected gift and the small gesture gave him an extraordinary amount of pleasure. 'And her surname.'

'Larson.'

Chloe's name. Not his.

The doctor on duty came into the bay, putting an end to that conversation. He engaged

Lily in a discussion about the plaster he was about to apply as Chloe took the clipboard and forms from Xander and swiftly completed them.

'What colour would you like your plaster to be?' the doctor was asking. 'Would you like pink?'

Lily shook her head. 'Green.'

Like Anna's dress, Xander thought. He may not know everything about Lily but he knew her favourite colour. And the more time he spent with her, the better he would know her. He just hoped he would have as much time as he wanted.

Lily was asleep in the car, her green, plastered arm cradled in her lap. Xander was driving but Chloe noticed that he was constantly glancing in the rearview mirror, checking on Lily.

'I felt so useless today when I couldn't fill out those forms,' he said as he returned his gaze to the road. 'It made me realise how much I've missed, how little I know about her.'

'She's only young,' Chloe said. 'There's plenty of time if you want to be involved in her life.'

'She's taken her first step, got her first tooth, said her first word. You got to see her first smile. She's had her first day at nursery. There's a lot to make up.'

Chloe didn't want to argue; this day had been stressful enough, and she knew he was right. She tried to placate him. 'She still has to have her first day at school, lose her first tooth, have her first boyfriend. She'll need someone to teach her how to drive a car.'

'Those things are all in the future. I've missed her past. I've missed three birthdays, three Christmases, three father's days. I missed her birth.'

'Xander, I said I'm sorry. I *did* try.'

'I know. I'm not blaming you for that.'

Was he blaming her for everything that came after that though?

'She was born at 6:52 in the morning,' Chloe told him. She didn't know if he wanted a description of the day Lily was born but perhaps it would help him. 'She was six weeks premature. I was terrified when I went into labour. Despite my training I had no idea how it would end. I'd had none of the risk factors for early delivery and my mother had had no problems with any of her pregnancies either. I was worried that something was wrong with Lily. With me.

'She spent a week in the NICU and three weeks in hospital. But she's a fighter, a survivor. She progressed really well and she's meeting all her milestones but it was a scary time. I think partly because I knew all the things that could go wrong and I worried about every last one of them. I wish you'd been there. I could have used your calm head.'

'I don't know how calm I would have been.'

'Are you kidding? You're so good in a crisis.'

'It's always different when it's personal.'

'You were good today. I don't know what I would have done without you. She is everything to me,' Chloe said as Xander turned the car into her street.

She unlocked the front door and let Xander carry Lily inside and she felt the tears well in her eyes as she looked at Xander with the tiny, precious bundle in his arms.

Her mother met them in the hall, alerted to their arrival by the sound of Chloe's key in the lock.

'Oh, the poor darling.'

'She's okay, Mum, but I'm going to put her straight to bed.' She looked at Xander. 'Can you give me a few minutes?' She needed some time to compose herself.

Chloe took Lily from his arms, dismissing him, and the loss of her weight felt like an ache in his heart.

He could feel Chloe's mother watching him and he tried to keep his expression neutral. It had been a stressful day and he could feel his emotions bubbling close to the surface. He needed to hold it together. He needed to stay strong.

'Come and wait with me, Xander,' Susan offered. 'I'll put the kettle on.'

He could use something stronger, he thought as he waited for the water to boil while he filled Susan in on the details of Lily's accident.

'How was your day until then?' she asked.

'I'm not sure,' he admitted. There had been patches where he'd felt they were both relaxed and shared some easy conversation, a few connected moments, but there'd been times he thought that Chloe was holding something back too. 'Chloe says you raised her and her brothers on your own. I don't know if she thinks I'm needed.' That was his main concern. That Chloe didn't need him.

'I'm not sure I'm the one you should be having this conversation with,' Susan said as she warmed the teapot. 'I didn't choose to raise my kids by myself but I managed. I raised them on my own because my husband left me with no choice.'

He thought that was an odd turn of phrase.

'Has Chloe told you anything about him?' Susan continued.

'She said he was a policeman and that he was killed in the line of duty.'

'That's true, but there's more to the reason why I raised my kids alone. Grant had an affair and left me. I struggled for a while before I pulled myself together for the sake of the kids. My mum came and stayed. Chloe was seven, old enough to remember, and she's never forgiven her father. She finds it difficult to put her trust in people.'

'In me.'

'Not just you,' Susan said as she poured the tea.

'I feel like she's giving me small bits of information, not the whole story.'

'It hasn't helped that she couldn't ever find you. It made her second-guess everything. She wondered if you knew she was looking for you, if anyone she spoke to who had worked with you ever passed on a message to you and if you just ignored that.'

Xander shook his head. 'I never knew.'

'You need to make that clear to her. You need to figure out what you want to do.'

'What do you mean?'

'You have lots of options. I'm not someone who thinks every child needs two parents.

Every circumstance is different and if you've got a parent who isn't invested in their child, then that's no better than only having one. Children need as much love as they can get. If you love them, you'll do your best by them and that's all anyone can expect. Chloe loves Lily. Adores her. She has been her world for the past three years. Longer, really. From the moment Chloe realised she was pregnant Lily has been her priority.

'She and Lily have my support and the support of Chloe's brothers but I know Chloe's choice would be for Lily to have two parents who love her equally. But there is nothing to say you have to be involved in Lily's life or that you have to do things Chloe's way but I will ask you this—please think very carefully before you disrupt their lives. Chloe's or Lily's. And you need to expect that it will take time for her to adjust to sharing Lily. If that's what you want.'

Xander was still mulling over Susan's advice when Chloe reappeared.

'How is she?' Susan asked.

'She's okay. She woke up but she's gone back to sleep now. I expect we'll have a restless night.'

'You already look exhausted,' Xander said.

'Thank you.' She gave him a tired smile. 'Always nice to hear I look as bad as I feel.'

'I didn't mean that.' In his opinion she still looked beautiful but her skin was so pale it was almost translucent and there were dark purple shadows under her eyes. The day had taken its toll on all of them. It had been stressful, emotionally charged, and it hadn't ended the way any of them had expected.

Chloe collapsed onto a chair as Susan excused herself. Leaving them alone.

'Lily didn't ask for me when she woke up?' Xander asked as he picked up the teapot and poured Chloe a cup.

Chloe sighed. 'She's met you twice, Xander. She doesn't know you yet. Give her time.'

She was right. It was going to take more than a weekend for Lily to bond with him. For her to get used to him being around. And it wasn't only Lily who needed to learn he could be trusted. Who needed time. Chloe needed that too.

He wanted to be part of her life. Their lives. Chloe's and Lily's.

It didn't matter if Lily was his biological child or not.

She might be the only child he ever had and Chloe's word was good enough for him. He didn't want to muck things up.

Mindful of Susan's words, he knew he needed to find out what Chloe wanted. What she needed. He couldn't afford to make a mistake.

'I want to be part of Lily's life. I want her to know who I am. But I also need to know what you want. We're in this together. We need to work out how we do this going forward.' He needed a plan. He needed to prove to Chloe that his intentions were true. That he wasn't going to disappear again. He needed to make plans to stay. 'Tell me what you want.'

'I'm not sure.'

'What did you want when you found out you were pregnant? What did you want when you looked for me?'

'I dreamt of a life with you but that was a fantasy. It wasn't reality. I thought you didn't want children so I convinced myself that it was better that I couldn't find you. Then I didn't have to listen to your side of the argument.'

'But I do want children and if I am Lily's father I want to be part of her life. And yours. I think we both need some time to work out what that means.'

Even before he saw Chloe unsuccessfully try to stifle a yawn he knew they weren't going to solve their issues tonight. The conversation needed fresh heads and clear minds.

'We can talk about this later. It looks like you need to go to bed. Will you let me know how Lily is in the morning?'

'Of course.'

She walked with him to the front door.

He kissed her on the forehead and wondered where they would go from here as he said goodnight.

Chloe watched him walk away.

He wanted to be part of her life but what did that mean exactly? He was Lily's father and nothing would take that away from him but how did she fit in? What did their future look like in his eyes? Did he want her?

He had said he would like to get married again. What if he married someone else? Lily would spend half the time with him and a stepmother. That wasn't the life she wanted for her daughter.

That wasn't the life she wanted for herself.

She wanted to share her life with someone too.

She wanted Lily to have her father. She wanted someone to love Lily.

She wanted someone to love her.

She wanted Xander.

She sighed and wiped a stray tear from her eye as she closed the door. She still loved him. Had he ever loved her?

CHAPTER TEN

'HI. THIS IS a nice surprise.' Xander answered his door to find Chloe outside. He had spoken to her but hadn't seen her for a couple of days. She had taken time off work so she could keep Lily at home and keep her quiet for forty-eight hours following her accident. 'Come in. How are you? How's Lily?'

'She's perfectly fine. She's home with my mum today but she's not complaining of any pain.' She stepped inside but stopped beside the small table in his entryway. 'Are these the DNA tests?' she asked.

Xander had left the addressed envelope lying on the table. He nodded.

'Have you done your test?'

He nodded again.

'But you haven't sent it off?'

'No.' He walked past the table and Chloe followed him into the lounge.

'Why not?' she asked as she sat down.

'Because I don't need to know the results. I don't care. I want her to be mine.'

'She is yours.'

But he'd been afraid of what might happen if the results said otherwise. That was why the envelope remained unsent. He wanted Lily to be his daughter so badly. Chloe had sworn she was and his fertility tests confirmed she could be. That was enough for him.

Chloe was holding out her hand. She held a USB stick between her thumb and forefinger. 'I brought you something. A peace offering. It's some photos of Lily. Of some of the moments you've missed.'

'Thank you.' He had missed so much, he thought as he took the gift. Three years. He wondered if Lily would feel the same sense of loss. 'Do you think she's missed having me in her life?' he asked as he led her into the living room.

'I've tried to do my best.'

'You've done a brilliant job,' he said. 'She's gorgeous, bright, inquisitive, friendly and confident.'

'I honestly think that if you're prepared to be part of her life from now on that will be enough. She's young. She's not going to remember these years. They're formative but she's had good role models, lots of love.

That's what she's needed. I don't think she's missed out.'

'But I feel like I have.'

'I know. And I'm sorry. I really did try to find you but when I couldn't I started to worry. I didn't really know you. I had no idea how you felt about kids. All I knew was that your divorce had knocked you for six. I wasn't sure if you'd want anything to do with us and I started to think you were avoiding my attempts to get in touch. Maybe I should have tried harder.' Chloe sat on the couch, her arms crossed defensively over her chest.

'I wasn't avoiding you,' he said as he put the USB stick down and reached for Chloe's hands, trying to encourage her to relax. 'I didn't know you were trying to find me. When you left I was miserable. Everywhere I looked, everywhere I went, I was reminded of you and it was horrible. I was happy while you were there and then you were gone. I didn't want to be there any more so I left. I needed to get away from all the memories.'

'You didn't think to come to find *me*? Why spend all that time travelling the world and not come here?'

'You were young and gorgeous, happy to have a working holiday romance. What could you possibly want with a grumpy old man?'

'You weren't old.' Chloe smiled. 'And you weren't always grumpy.'

'I was a miserable old man.' He could smile about it now. That man was gone, thanks to Chloe. His future was full of possibility. 'You had your whole life ahead of you. I had a broken marriage and health issues. We had four weeks together. I didn't know how you felt and I didn't know what my future held. I didn't know what my prognosis was at that stage and it wasn't fair to think you might want to take a chance on a man who may have only a few years left. I figured eventually I'd find a place where I was happy again. I couldn't come for you. I had nothing to offer you then.'

'And now?'

'Now I'm thinking what an idiot I was and how much time I've wasted. But hindsight is a wonderful thing. I should have listened to my heart four years ago but I listened to my head instead and I've been searching for happiness ever since. I've found it again. With you. We can make this work.'

'Make what work?'

'You. Me. Lily.'

'How?'

'I could stay here,' he said. 'I've had a long journey to get here but I feel like this is where

I am meant to be. With you. We will figure this out.'

He'd given this a lot of thought over the past few days but he needed to know where Chloe stood.

Xander reached one hand towards her and Chloe could feel herself being seduced by his words. By the picture he was painting. By the earnestness she could see in his grey eyes.

Did he really want to be with her?

Would he stay?

Could she trust him?

His fingers skimmed her jaw and slid into her hair. His thumb stroked her skin. Waves of desire washed over her and she forgot about his promises. It took all her concentration to remember just to breathe. Her life might have changed—her life was no longer simple and carefree—but her reaction to Xander remained constant.

The touch of his fingertips on her bare skin sent a buzz of anticipation straight to her groin and she felt as though she was on fire. She rested her head back on the couch, relishing the sensation as his touch brought her body to life.

He leant towards her. He was inches from her, his lips close enough to kiss, his neck close enough to nestle into. She breathed in deeply, savouring his smell.

She met him halfway, closing her eyes as his lips touched hers. She heard her soft moan as he kissed her. She parted her lips, welcoming his tongue into her mouth. Letting him explore her and taste her as she tasted him.

His hand was on her hip and he lifted her easily and pulled her onto his lap. She felt his hand slide up under her shirt, warm against her back, but his lips didn't leave hers. Her hands wound around his neck as he undid her bra with a flick of his fingers.

She arched her back as his fingers traced her ribcage. She gasped as his fingers cupped the underside of her breast and her nipple hardened in expectation as his thumb stroked her flesh. He found her nipple, stopping to tease it, running his thumb over and around it, sending electric shocks through her body.

His hands moved to her waist and Chloe lifted her arms above her head as he removed her clothes. He trailed a line of kisses down her neck to her breasts and ran his tongue across one nipple, turning her dizzy with desire before he took her other breast into his mouth, sucking it and making her writhe in ecstasy. She pushed her hips towards him, unable to keep still.

She needed him to touch her. She needed to feel his hands on her. She couldn't think beyond where his fingers might land next. Where she might next feel his mouth on her skin. She was consumed by need. By passion.

She reached for him now, her hands reading her mind. Reaching for his shirt she pulled it free from his pants, running her fingers over his skin, feeling the heat radiating from him. She undid his belt and her fingers fumbled with the button on his waistband. He lifted his hips and, with one hand, pushed his trousers down without moving her off his lap.

Chloe knew where this night would end—there was no denying that, just as there was no denying she wanted it as badly as she'd wanted anything in her entire life. As far as she was concerned, she was his for the taking. She knew she'd wanted this since the moment he'd reappeared in her life. She didn't care that her life had moved on. She no longer cared where he'd been for the last few years. All she cared about was feeling his hands on her again, his lips on hers, having him inside her once again. She'd worry about what happened next another time. There was no room in her head for anything else.

His hand was on her belly and then his fingers slid beneath, under the elastic of her underwear, and rested between her thighs, covering her most sensitive spot. A place that felt like the centre of the universe. He slid one finger inside her and Chloe closed her eyes, almost unable to bear the waves of desire crashing through her. Heat flooded through her and she tore open the buttons on his shirt and pushed it aside, pressing herself against him, chest to chest, skin to skin, as his fingers continued to work their magic, bringing her to a peak of pleasure. She threw her head back as she thrust her hips towards him and just when she thought she was about to explode he paused.

She opened her eyes and she saw the question in his face. She didn't want him to stop; there was only one conclusion she could bear to have.

She wanted him unable to resist, she wanted him at her mercy and she wanted him inside her. She pulled his head down to her and kissed him hard, wondering at what point she had become the leader. She broke away, biting his lip gently between her teeth before lifting her head. She wanted to watch him, wanted to see his expression as she took control.

She pushed his boxer shorts down over his hips, freeing him, and closed her hand around his shaft. He was fully aroused, firm and warm in her hand, and as she ran her fingers up his shaft and across the sensitive tip she heard him gasp with pleasure. His lips were parted, his grey eyes dark, his breathing rapid.

'Wait.' His voice was deep and hoarse, as if he could barely summon the energy to speak. He gave her a half-smile. 'I guess we need some protection.'

Her bag lay on the floor beside the couch and she reached for it, opening her purse and finding a condom.

'You carry them with you?'

'Perks of the job.' She smiled as she tore open the packet and rolled the condom onto him.

She pushed him backwards slightly, adjusting her hips before she brought him back to her and guided him inside. She welcomed him in and wrapped her legs around him to keep him close. He closed his eyes and a sigh of pleasure escaped his lips. She lifted her hips, pushing him deeper inside her, and closed her eyes too as she listened to him moan in delight. She concentrated on the rhythm of movement, the sensation of their bodies joined together as he thrust into her.

But he wasn't to be outdone. He found a gap between their hips and with one hand he stroked the source of her pleasure. His fingers moved in small, soft circles that almost brought her undone.

She heard his name on her lips as he thrust inside her, as his fingers continued their magic, bringing her to a peak of excitement.

'Now, please,' she begged for release. She couldn't hold on any longer. Her head was thrown back and Xander dropped his head to her breast, sucking on a nipple. She lifted her hands to his head, holding on to his hair, keeping his head down as he brought her to a climax. Her entire body shuddered and, as she felt her orgasm peak, she felt Xander's release too.

They collapsed in each other's arms, spent and satisfied.

It felt as though it had been only days since their bodies had known each other. The memory of their time together imprinted on every nerve ending, every cell, coming back without hesitation. But Chloe knew time had taken its toll. No matter how she felt. No matter how intense their chemistry was, nothing about this situation was simple.

Chloe stepped out of the shower, dried herself off and reluctantly got dressed. Xander had gone back to work for a training session and she needed to get home.

Her whole body still tingled. Their chemistry was still amazing. It hadn't diminished and the more she learned about him, the closer she felt, and that added another layer, another dimension, to their lovemaking.

But amazing chemistry wasn't the solution to their issues. They really needed to have a discussion about what happened next. He was insistent that they could make things work but he didn't live here. His time in London was drawing to a close and then what would happen? She didn't know if his comment about staying in London was serious. Was that really his plan? And what would that mean for Lily going forward?

They hadn't even told Lily who he was yet. She had argued that Lily was young and it would confuse her. She'd wanted Lily to have time with Xander, a chance to get to know him before they thrust big changes on her. But she knew it was more about her resistance. Her own hesitance. She'd wanted more time herself. She didn't know what changes she could cope with.

She'd had three years to work out what she would do if, when, she found Xander and still she didn't know. The reality was that three years wasn't long enough to figure it out and six weeks definitely wasn't long enough.

Could they have a future? she wondered as she picked up her bag. He certainly seemed to think so but she was more pessimistic. She didn't believe in everlasting love. But she was willing to see where this would go. For Lily's sake.

For hers.

No one had ever made her feel like Xander had and she didn't want to regret letting him go again.

She opened his front door, noticing again the envelope sitting on the hall table. She slipped it into her bag. She would post it. She wanted him to see the results for himself. She thought it was important.

Chloe lay curled against Xander's side revelling in the fact that she could stay the night. Lily wouldn't miss her. She was used to Chloe working night shifts and leaving her in Susan's care and Chloe had no idea how many more opportunities she'd get to lie in Xander's arms. She didn't want to miss any of them.

She lay with her head against his chest and listened to the rhythm of his heart and let the waves of contentment wash over her. She closed her eyes and relaxed into the peace and comfort of his embrace.

'What are you thinking about?' His voice rumbled under her ear.

'About one of the last times I spent the night with you. How peaceful I felt. I feel like that now.'

'Which night was it?'

'Your thirtieth birthday. Do you remember where we were?'

'At Uluru.'

Chloe nodded. It had been their last weekend together before she had left Australia. 'I think that was the most peaceful place I've ever been.' They had walked around the base of the massive red rock and watched the colours change as the sun set over the ancient land. They had made love under the stars and had walked through Kata Tjuta the next morning. The weekend was everything she'd imagined it to be but a hundred times better because she was spending it with him. She had known her time was ending, that she would soon be leaving, so she made sure to savour every detail, making memories she could take home with her. 'There was something special about that country. Something more than the space and the colours and the stars. It was spiritual. Did you feel it? Something was at work there. Something bigger than us. Something powerful.'

Xander looked sideways at her. 'Why do you say that?'

'I think that's when I fell pregnant.'

'I still can't get my head around the idea that my ex-wife and I had trouble conceiving *before* I had cancer but after my treatment, when I had all but given up on the idea, you fell pregnant in the blink of an eye.'

'I think it was meant to be.'

'Fate?'

Chloe shook her head. 'It was more than that. I felt spirits.' Walking through Kata Tjuta she had felt that they weren't alone. That they were being watched. There hadn't been a breath of wind, nor a sound. There had been not another soul in sight but she hadn't been able to shake the feeling that they were not alone. 'I'm not a religious person by any means but I can only describe what I felt as something spiritual and extraordinarily peaceful.'

'Spirits?'

She nodded, waiting to see if he was going to laugh at her idea but he surprised her when he asked, 'Why would they give us a baby?'

She'd thought a lot about this over the past four years.

'I think I needed someone to love. I think you did too. But fate, or the spirits, forgot to factor in that I was leaving soon. Maybe it was just science. Maybe it was as simple as the pill I forgot to take and the fact that you recovered quickly, but I still feel there was more at play. I thought there was a reason it had happened.'

'You missed a pill?'

She nodded. 'I always take one in the morning, but when I went to get it out of my bag, I found I forgot to pack them. We were literally in the middle of the desert, so there was nothing I could do about it. I didn't think it would matter—we were using protection as well but I guess condoms really are only ninety-nine per cent effective. I think someone, somewhere, really wanted me pregnant.'

'You can thank the spirits,' Xander said, 'but I call it fate. And now fate has brought us together again. I just wish we'd had the last four years as well.'

'Do you think we would have lasted if we'd spent every day together?'

'I do.' He smiled and flipped her onto her back. He lifted her into the centre of the bed and spread her legs before running his fingers up the inside of her thigh. 'Let me show you why,' he said as he pulled her hips towards him.

Chloe sighed and arched her back as she felt his warm breath between her thighs.

Right now, she would believe anything he

told her. She didn't even care if they didn't have for ever. She'd got over him once before and she knew she could do it again if she had to.

CHAPTER ELEVEN

THE WEDDING HAD been beautiful and Chloe hoped that Esther and Harry would prove her wrong. She really hoped they would get their happily ever after. She realised there were no guarantees but she'd be happy to bet on Esther and Harry making the distance.

She'd enjoyed the day. The weather had been glorious, perfect for a wedding in an historic mansion, and their vows had been genuine and heartfelt and had made plenty of the guests emotional. And dinner had been divine, the speeches both entertaining and moving, and the bride looked stunning.

Chloe was already looking forward to the next wedding, to Carly and Adem's special day, not least because it would mean Izzy was back as well. She was excited to think that the four of them—Carly, Esther, Izzy and herself—would be able to spend time together. She knew things were different now—

Esther was married and Carly would soon be a wife *and* a mother—but even though their focus had shifted Chloe knew the four of them would always be in each other's lives. She could count on them.

She let her gaze wander across the room, towards Xander. She had tried to concentrate on being a good bridesmaid, and she hoped she'd done her duty, but she'd been constantly on the lookout for Xander. Always aware of where he was. And whenever she looked in his direction she found he was watching her. He would wink or smile at her and she glowed in the attention.

The wedding had been fabulous but she was ready to leave now. She was ready to go home with Xander. Her mum was looking after Lily and Chloe wasn't expected home until tomorrow.

He looked handsome in a dark, charcoal grey suit, with a fine white stripe. The colour highlighted both his tan and his grey eyes. She still got goosebumps when she looked at him and his touch continued to make her heart beat faster and her breath catch.

Could she count on him?

Could Lily?

They really needed to have a discussion about what happened next. He had mentioned leaving and he had mentioned staying but he'd said nothing about either option lately and she didn't know what he was planning on doing next. She had no idea but she couldn't continue to ignore the fact that he didn't live here and his six weeks were almost at an end.

He was walking towards her. His eyes did not leave hers as he crossed the room. She waited for him. Knowing he was coming for her. His gaze pinning her to the spot.

'Can I drag you away from your bridesmaid's duties for a moment?'

He took her hand and she couldn't think. She couldn't speak. All she could do was follow him outside onto the terrace.

'There's something I need to ask you,' he said.

Fairy lights glowed in the garden around them as he sat her down and then sat beside her.

'Chloe?'

It was a magical, romantic setting and Chloe's breath caught in her throat. 'Yes.'

'I want to tell Lily that I am her father,' he said. 'It's time.'

'Have you got the DNA results back?'

He nodded and withdrew an envelope from his jacket pocket.

Chloe swallowed, suddenly nervous, even though she knew what the results would show.

'And? What do they say?'

'I don't know. I haven't opened them.'

Chloe stared at the envelope that Xander held between his fingers as if she could see through it and read the writing inside. 'Why not?'

'Because I don't need to. Because in my heart I know she's mine,' he said as he tore the envelope in two and put it back in his pocket.

'What are you doing?'

'Lily is our daughter, Chloe. I don't need a piece of paper to tell me that. I trust you and I believe you. I know she's mine and now I want to tell her who I am.'

She nodded. He was right. It was time. She couldn't deny him this any longer. Lily deserved to know the truth too and then they'd have to work out what happened next. 'When do you want to tell her?'

'I want to come home with you tomorrow. I'm going back to Australia next week. My parents are celebrating their fortieth wedding anniversary and my sisters want me there. They've insisted. I want to take Lily with me.'

'You want to do what?' Chloe felt her surroundings sway. She had spots in her peripheral vision and Xander faded in and out of focus. She wasn't sure if she was going to faint or vomit. He *couldn't* take her. 'You want to take her away?'

This was *not* part of the plan.

'I'm not taking her away but I want her to meet my side of the family—'

'Chloe! There you are.' Carly stepped onto the deck and spotted Chloe and Xander. 'I've been looking everywhere for you. Esther and Harry are leaving and I thought you'd want to say goodbye.' She was greeted with silence and stony expressions. She looked from Chloe to Xander and back again. 'Am I interrupting?'

'No,' Chloe said. She'd heard enough. 'We're finished.' She stood up and followed Carly back inside, ready to farewell the bride and groom.

Chloe stood with Carly as they waved Esther and Harry off. The minute the newlyweds had departed Adem came and claimed Carly for one last dance, leaving Chloe on the sidelines. She had never felt more alone than she did right now.

'Chloe.' Xander materialised beside her. 'Please, you need to listen to me. There's more to explain.' His grey eyes were dark, anxious. What more could he have to say? Was that why he'd gone quiet about his plans recently? Because he'd been intending to take Lily away? She never should have trusted him.

'I'm tired. It's been a long day and I want to go home.' She was close to tears and she really didn't think she had the energy to deal with anything unpleasant.

'Please. Just give me ten minutes. It's important.'

She sighed. She could tell from the set of his shoulders, from the shadows in his eyes, that he wasn't going to let this go. 'Ten minutes,' she replied, and let him guide her back out to the terrace, away from the other guests.

'I don't want to take Lily to Australia by herself,' he said when they were outside again. 'She is still getting to know me. I want you to come too.'

'Me?'

'Of course. I couldn't take Lily to the other side of the world without her mum. I thought we could make it a family trip.'

'But we're not a family,' she argued.

'Not yet,' he said as he got her to sit down, 'but I'd like us to be. People have told me you don't miss what you've never had but I never believed that. I missed being a father but missing fatherhood was nothing compared to finding out I have a daughter and knowing that I could miss out on her life, on watching her grow up. There is no way I'm walking away from Lily. Or from you. I want us to be a family.'

He knelt down beside her and said, 'I want you to marry me.'

'What?'

'Marry me. Make us a family.'

She was shaking as she said, 'I can't marry you.'

'Why not?'

'It's too soon.' Her heart was racing. It was too fast, one beat merging with the next. She couldn't breathe. Couldn't think. Couldn't see.

'How do you figure that?'

She swallowed and took several deep breaths as she tried to slow her heart rate. Tried to stop her hands from shaking. 'We've known each other for eight weeks and half of those weeks were four years ago. We know nothing about each other. Not really.'

'I know we have amazing chemistry.'

Chloe shook her head. 'Passion like that isn't sustainable. It would burn out and then what would we be left with? We'd be two strangers who had a child together.'

'You can't believe that.' He held her hands in his and finally the shakes subsided. 'We are so much more than two people. We are two halves. We're meant to be together. I know you feel it too.' He lifted her hands to his mouth and kissed her fingers. 'I should have asked you to stay all those years ago. We could have avoided all of this. We could have been together.'

'But you didn't.' She had waited for him to ask. She would have stayed if he had asked her to. But he'd said nothing. Done nothing and so she'd left. Nursing her heart. Carrying her secret.

'I couldn't. I had nothing to offer you. My life had not gone in the direction I had hoped and I was struggling to process all of that. I was recently divorced and waiting for that magical five years post-diagnosis. I was damaged. Hurting. I was angry.'

'Were you still in love with your wife? Did she break your heart?'

'No. She didn't break my heart. My ego was bruised. I was disappointed and damaged. I grew up in a close-knit family and I always imagined I would have that too. That was how I pictured my life. A wife and kids. I know I rushed into my first marriage. I was caught up in living my dream and when it came crashing down, instead of turning to my family for support I turned away. I couldn't handle watching their happy lives. I had a lot of soul searching to do. I've spent years trying to find meaning in my life, trying to tell myself that I loved my job and that was enough for me. That it was fulfilling. And it is, in its way, but it's not enough. I need more. I need you.

'I didn't fall in love with my first wife across a crowded room but you took my breath away the moment I saw you. I felt an instant connection. I was sad when my marriage ended. I was disappointed, lost, but I was adrift when you left me.

'She bruised my heart, you repaired it. She damaged my spirit and you healed it but then I let you go. I'm not going to make the same mistake twice. I want to spend the rest of my life with you. I love you. Marry me, Chloe. Be my wife.'

This was what she wanted but she couldn't let herself believe that it could be her life. That she could be happy. That she could get the ending she had dreamt of. 'We don't have to get married.'

'I want to.'

'Marriage is just a piece of paper.'

'Not to me,' he said.

'How can you say that? You've already been divorced once.'

'That wasn't my doing. I took my marriage vows seriously but I couldn't stay married. Her affair was a deal breaker. But I'm not sorry that I got divorced. It left me free to meet you. I didn't think I'd be lucky enough to find another person I could love and then I didn't realise it was you until you'd gone. I let you go once and I'm not going to let you go a second time. I couldn't be lucky enough to find you a third time. I don't believe in coincidences but there's a higher power working for us. We'd be silly to ignore it. I love you, Chloe. Do you love me?'

'I'm scared.'

'Of what?'

'Of giving you my heart and it not working out. Of you making promises that you might not be able to keep. Of you feeling like you have to marry me because we have a child together. I've seen it all before. It doesn't work.'

'Is this about your parents?'

She nodded. 'They got married because of me. And they shouldn't have.'

'What happened between them?'

She took a deep breath. It was time to tell him everything. Time to expose all the secrets. Maybe then she could move forward.

'My father had just broken up with his girlfriend when he started dating my mother. She fell pregnant unexpectedly and my father did the "right thing" and married her. In hindsight that was a mistake. A pretty big one. They stayed together for a few years, long enough to have my brothers as well. Long enough to make things really difficult for Mum when Dad left.

'He moved out just after Tom was born. Apparently he'd started seeing his old girlfriend again, the one he'd broken up with before he met Mum. He said he'd never got over her and if Mum hadn't got pregnant he would never have married her but would probably have patched things up with his ex. I don't understand why he waited so long to call it quits. I get that he thought he was doing the right thing, but he shouldn't have made a life with Mum, shouldn't have spent all those years with us, only to leave. He left us all. Just walked out. And then he was killed before they got divorced but I can't forgive him for leaving us in the first place.

'And so, you see, I don't believe people are truly capable of making a commitment to each other and keeping it. I think we're setting ourselves up to fail. Even if one person is committed, it takes two. Even if they're in love it isn't always enough to keep a marriage going and a child is no guarantee either. When I found out I was pregnant I dreamt of finding you and of us being able to work it all out but I never really believed it. I would never have pressured you into anything but I must admit I did, briefly, imagine a happy family situation, but I realised there are no guarantees of that. We had insane chemistry but I knew that wasn't enough.'

'I promise you, I'm not going anywhere. I won't leave you.'

'You're going home,' she said.

'Home?'

'To Australia.'

He shook his head. 'That's just for a visit. I want to introduce my family to you and Lily. Home is where you are. My two girls. I've applied for a permanent position here, with the air ambulance service. Eloise has resigned. She and her husband are moving to Spain. My maternal grandmother was English. I can stay here. With you. I want us to be a family. You, me, Lily. From the moment I saw her I knew she was mine. She's a miracle. My miracle. The child I thought I'd never have. But even if she wasn't biologically mine I wouldn't care. She's a part of you and that's enough for me. I'm not asking you to marry me out of obligation. I'm asking because I love you.'

He placed her hand on her chest, over her own heart and wrapped his arms around her. 'Close your eyes and tell me how you feel.'

She had fallen hard for him four years ago

but she'd convinced herself that such powerful feelings couldn't last. They would have to burn out. People fell in love all the time but obviously those feelings didn't last, otherwise there wouldn't be divorces. But Xander had already been divorced—if he still believed in love and marriage maybe she could too. She closed her eyes and listened to his heartbeat keeping time with her own. 'I feel safe,' she said. 'I feel like I'm where I'm supposed to be.'

'Trust your heart,' he said as she opened her eyes.

'It's not my heart that's the problem. It's my head. I have spent years believing that true love can't last but you make me want to change my mind.'

'What do you mean?'

'I fell in love with you all those years ago but I talked myself out of it.'

'You loved me?' he asked. 'Could you love me again?' he asked when she nodded.

'I never stopped loving you,' she told him. 'But I don't know if love is enough.'

'Of course it is. What else is there? What we have is special. I can't compare it to anything else I've known. Trust me on this. We can make this work. I haven't felt like this in four years. Maybe ever. I feel at peace. It's not a coincidence that you fell pregnant. It's not a coincidence that we found each other again. It's fate. We are meant to be together. I love you. I love our daughter and I want us to be a family. Please believe in me. Believe in us. Will you be my wife? Will you marry me?'

She loved him. She knew that much.

She'd been waiting for him all her life.

This was her chance. She had to take it. She had to trust him. She had to trust in them.

'Yes,' she said as she kissed him. 'I love you and I will marry you.'

EPILOGUE

CHLOE SAT IN an upholstered tub chair and gazed out of the window. She felt as if she was living in a dream. This morning she had woken up in London, and now here she was, fourteen hours later, sitting in a hotel room in France looking out at the lights and turrets of a make-believe castle.

They were fifty kilometres east of Paris but she felt as though she'd been transported into her own personal fairy tale. It felt like a dream and she knew that was what the creators of this fantasyland were trying to achieve; she just hadn't expected it to be so effective.

She watched as Xander opened the doors onto the Juliet balcony and the curtains billowed in the spring evening breeze, bringing in the scent of jasmine.

She jumped, startled out of her reverie, as Xander popped the cork on a bottle of champagne.

'I don't have any gin but I thought champagne was a more fitting way to celebrate our engagement,' he said as he poured two glasses and handed her one just as the first firework burst in the sky above the iconic castle.

Chloe gasped. 'I had no idea we'd be able to see the fireworks from our room. Did you book this especially?'

He nodded. 'Do you like it?' He looked well pleased with himself, as he should—the view was spectacular.

'I love it! Lily would too.'

'Shall we wake her up?'

Chloe shook her head. Lily was fast asleep in an adjoining bedroom. She was exhausted from the travel today and then an afternoon spent exploring the theme park and racing from one magical princess-themed ride to another. Although admittedly she had barely walked—Xander, a devoted father, had carried her on his shoulders for most of the day— but Chloe didn't want to spoil tomorrow by having an overwrought three-year-old to deal with. 'No. She can watch them tomorrow. She'll be unbearable then if she gets up now and I want her, want *all* of us, to enjoy the princess breakfast you've booked.'

'To tomorrow.' Xander tapped his champagne flute against Chloe's and reached for her hand. He pulled her off her seat and into his lap. She nestled against him and sipped her champagne as the last fireworks lit up the sky and the clock edged towards tomorrow.

'Good morning, Your Royal Highnesses. Sleeping Beauty. Anna.'

Chloe sat up to find Xander standing at the foot of her bed, which she'd climbed into in the early hours of the morning so that Lily didn't find her in the bed next door, with Xander. There was time enough for that once they were married.

In the bed beside her Lily sat up, rubbing her eyes. 'Who's Anna?'

'You, of course, Your Majesty,' Xander replied as Lily giggled.

'Why are you dressed like that?' she asked.

He was wearing a pair of black trousers with a white shirt. There was nothing startling about that, but over the top he had a jacket in a royal blue fabric with gold buttons and heavy gold embroidery. He had a frilled collar placed over the front of his shirt. He looked like a footman from any number of Disney movies.

He placed a tray on the bedside table as he said, 'Every princess gets a hot drink brought to them in the morning by the royal tea maker. A cup of tea for you, Sleeping Beauty, and a hot chocolate for Princess Anna,' he said as he handed out mugs. 'And then it's time to get ready for breakfast.'

'Is the princess breakfast today?' Lily squealed.

'It is. We have forty minutes to get dressed and be downstairs. Drink your hot chocolate and I will see to your clothes.'

'Where on earth did you get that jacket?' Chloe asked.

'Some mice made it for me in the night,' he replied with a wink before he spun around and left, going back through the door into the adjoining room. Chloe frowned—what was he up to? Lily's clothes were in the wardrobe in their room.

He returned seconds later and laid a garment bag across the foot of Lily's bed.

'What's in there?'

'If I told you that I'd ruin the surprise. All the princesses will be in their best dresses this morning and I thought Lily should have something new to wear too.'

'Is it for me?' she asked as Chloe reached over and took Lily's hot chocolate from her before her bouncing emptied the contents of the mug all over the bed, Lily and the bag.

'Can I open it?' Lily was clapping her hands with excitement.

Chloe nodded and Lily slid the zip down to reveal a dress with a dark green velvet bodice, soft cap sleeves and a pleated cream and green embroidered skirt.

'It's beautiful, Xander.'

Lily leapt up from the bed and threw her arms around Xander's neck. 'Thank you, Daddy, thank you!'

'You're welcome. I'll leave you to get ready,' he said, and as he turned for the door Chloe was almost certain she saw tears in his eyes.

Lily could barely stand still. Dressed in her costume she couldn't stop twirling around in circles as they waited in the line for breakfast. She had insisted on walking to the restaurant between Chloe and Xander, holding their hands, but the minute they got to the queue she had let go and Xander had slipped Chloe's hand into his instead.

The line moved forward, bringing them level with two thrones, a pink and gold one on their left and a red one to the right. A photographer was taking pictures, filling up time while people waited to be greeted by the hostess, who was dressed as Belle.

'*Bonjour!*' The photographer welcomed them and led them to a throne. '*Une famille très belle.*'

'Merci,' Xander said as Chloe beamed.

They were a family.

And their family was about to get bigger.

She smiled as the camera flashed, thinking of the news she planned to share with Xander tonight.

She kissed Xander's cheek as the camera flashed again, capturing the moment. She was getting her fairy-tale ending. Her own happily ever after.

She had everything she wished for.

* * * * *